Annie W
She Was Book
Fundraisers
Rodeo And Ranching,
Honky-Tonks And Country Music.

But their differences didn't seem to matter to his
libido when she wrapped her arms around his waist
and rested her head against his chest. Holding her
close was playing hell with his vow to keep his
distance, but he could no more step away from her
than a buffalo could roost in a tree. Something about
Annie made him want to make it up to her for her
lousy childhood, had him wanting to keep her from
ever being lonely again.

* * *

Dear Reader,

When it comes to passion, Silhouette Desire has exactly what you need. This month's offerings include Cindy Gerard's *The Librarian's Passionate Knight*, the next installment of DYNASTIES: THE BARONES. A naive librarian gets swept off her feet by a dashing Barone sibling—who could ask for anything more? But more we do have, with another story about attractive and wealthy men, from Anne Marie Winston. *Billionaire Bachelors: Gray* is a deeply compelling story about a man who gets a second chance at life—and maybe the love of a lifetime.

Sheri WhiteFeather is back this month with the final story in our LONE STAR COUNTRY CLUB trilogy. *The Heart of a Stranger* will leave you breathless when a man with a sordid past gets a chance for ultimate redemption. Launching a new series this month is Kathie DeNosky with *Lonetree Ranchers: Brant*. When a handsome rancher helps a damsel in distress, all his defenses come crashing down and the fun begins.

Silhouette Desire is pleased to welcome two brand-new authors. Nalini Singh's *Desert Warrior* is an intense, emotional read with an alpha hero to die for. And Anna DePalo's *Having the Tycoon's Baby*, part of our ongoing series THE BABY BANK, is a sexy romp about one woman's need for a child and the sexy man who grants her wish—but at a surprising price.

There's plenty of passion rising up here in Silhouette Desire this month. So dive right in and enjoy.

Melissa Jeglinski

Melissa Jeglinski
Senior Editor
Silhouette Desire

Please address questions and book requests to:
Silhouette Reader Service
U.S.: 3010 Walden Ave., P.O. Box 1325, Buffalo, NY 14269
Canadian: P.O. Box 609, Fort Erie, Ont. L2A 5X3

Lonetree
Ranchers: Brant
KATHIE DeNOSKY

Silhouette® Desire

Published by Silhouette Books
America's Publisher of Contemporary Romance

SILHOUETTE BOOKS

ISBN 0-373-76528-2

LONETREE RANCHERS: BRANT

Books by Kathie DeNosky

Silhouette Desire

Did You Say Married?! #1296
The Rough and Ready Rancher #1355
His Baby Surprise #1374
Maternally Yours #1418
Cassie's Cowboy Daddy #1439
Cowboy Boss #1457
A Lawman in Her Stocking #1475
In Bed with the Enemy #1521
Lonetree Ranchers: Brant #1528

KATHIE DeNOSKY

lives in her native southern Illinois with her husband, three children and one very spoiled dog. She writes highly sensual stories with a generous amount of humor. Kathie's books have appeared on the Waldenbooks bestseller list and received the Write Touch Readers' Award from WisRWA. She enjoys going to rodeos, traveling to research settings for her books and listening to country music. She often works through the night, so she can write without interruption, while the rest of the family is sleeping. You may contact Kathie at P.O. Box 2064, Herrin, Illinois 62948-5264 or e-mail her at kathie@kathiedenosky.com.

To professional rodeo bullfighter Joe Baumgartner,
for sharing his experiences and knowledge with me.

And a special thank-you to the Professional Bull Riders,
for showing me a behind-the-scenes look
at this exciting sport.

One

Her sensible black pumps held tightly in one hand, Anastasia Devereaux plastered her back to the brick wall behind her, took a deep breath and waited for the fog to clear from her glasses. "Don't look down," she whispered when the haze evaporated. "You can do this if you don't look down."

She closed her eyes in order to gather her courage and slow the erratic pounding of her heart. How on earth had she—an intelligent, totally unadventurous librarian—managed to find herself inching along the outside ledge surrounding the fourth floor of the Regal Suites Hotel in downtown Saint Louis? And at midnight, no less.

Glancing to her left, she gulped. There was no turning back now. If she did, she'd be trapped. She cautiously turned her head to the right. Her only option was to continue to the next balcony.

She took a deep breath and focused on the side of the building across the alley to keep from looking down as, inch by slow inch, she cautiously moved closer to the safety of the platform to her right. The rough brick behind her pulled at the twisted knot of hair at the back of her head, snagged her silk blouse and shredded the backs of her nylons. When the cold February wind whistled around her, she shivered. She wished she'd had the presence of mind to grab her coat and purse before she'd impulsively escaped Patrick's hotel room. But she hadn't, and there was no sense lamenting her shortsightedness now.

Her hip came into contact with the iron railing of the next balcony and she automatically reached out to wrap her hand around the cold metal. It felt like a lifeline and she held on for dear life as she tried to steady her frayed nerves. Her grandmother would never forgive her if she fell and her lifeless body was found in the Dumpster below. It would be terribly undignified. And a Whittmeyer woman—even one with the surname Devereaux—never lost her dignity. Ever.

"Forgive me, Grandmother, but there's no ladylike way to do this," Anastasia muttered as she tossed her shoes onto the balcony, then hitched up her khaki skirt to throw her leg over the wrought-iron railing.

Scrambling over the barrier, she fell onto the rough concrete floor. The surface bit into her knees and palms, but she ignored the pain. There was a light on inside and she thanked her lucky stars that she'd found her way to a room that was occupied. She prayed the person inside hadn't fallen asleep or gone out without turning off the lamp.

She gathered her shoes, took a deep breath and tentatively tapped on the sliding glass door. Silence.

Now what? Patrick could discover her missing at any moment, and if he walked out onto his balcony, he wouldn't have any trouble spotting her. Doubling her fist, she hoped the glass didn't break as she pounded on it for all she was worth. The sound of a muttered curse, then the slamming of a door was followed by silence.

"Please let me in," she called, feeling panic begin to claw at her insides.

"Where the hell are you?" a male voice inside the room shouted back. He didn't sound very sociable.

"I'm on the balcony. Please hurry," she added, glancing toward the platform outside Patrick's room.

When the drapes were suddenly yanked open, Anastasia blinked. She found herself staring through the glass at a man with the most extraordinary blue eyes, wearing nothing but a towel knotted at his waist and a formidable frown. Straight, sable-colored hair fell low on his forehead, softening his expression yet lending a ruggedness to his extremely handsome features that she found quite appealing.

She watched him disengage the lock and pull the door aside. "What the hell are you doing out there?" he demanded.

She dropped her shoes and took a step back. But her foot came down on one of the pumps and sent her reeling backward. The man lunged forward and, wrapping her securely in his arms, drew her to his bare chest before she toppled over the railing and fell to the alley below.

"Whoa there, sweetpea." His voice rumbled up from deep in his chest and sent an answering shiver straight up her spine. "That's a long way down and unless you're an angel with wings, I don't think doing a backflip off this balcony would be a real good idea."

"I don't." Anastasia shook her head. "Have wings, that is." She glanced over the wrought iron and shuddered at how close she'd come to falling. "And I'm afraid my landing would be anything but graceful."

The man continued to hold her as he backed them into the room and closed the balcony door. "You're safe now," he said, his voice suddenly sounding much more gentle than it had moments before.

A shiver coursed through her, but she wasn't sure if it was from being cold or the sound of his sexy baritone. And she couldn't discount the impressive muscles holding her to him, either. He had the widest shoulders and his chest looked exactly like the models on the boy-toy calendar her assistant, Tiffany, had tacked up in the storeroom at the library. The thought that the man holding her probably didn't have a stitch on beneath the towel caused her to shiver again.

"You're chilled to the bone, sweetpea," he said, obviously misinterpreting the reason for the tiny movement. His arms tightened around her.

This time she was sure the tremor running the length of her was due to the man holding her to him. Her cheek was pressed to his warm, bare chest and his hands were rubbing slow circles over her back. What woman with a pulse wouldn't shiver?

"Th-thank you…for letting me in."

"How long have you been out there?" he asked, his voice sending a fresh wave of goose bumps along her arms.

''I...I'm not sure.'' How long had she been out on that ledge? It seemed like hours, but it couldn't have been more than a few minutes. ''Five minutes. Maybe ten.''

As she continued to ponder the man's question, she realized he still held her firmly against his warm bare flesh. She pushed herself free, but the sight of blood on his smooth chest caused her to stop and glance down at her palms.

''Let me see,'' he said, taking her hands in his. He led her over to the bedside table and held them under the lamp for a better look. ''What happened?''

''I fell when...I climbed over the rail of the balcony,'' she said, realizing her knees were about to give way.

''How the hell did you get out there?''

''I walked—'' she shuddered at the thought of what she'd done ''—along the ledge.''

Whether it was the thought of how easily she could have fallen to her death or from the tingling sensation radiating where his warm hands held hers, she wasn't sure, but if she didn't sit down, and soon, she was in very real danger of falling on the floor at the man's big bare feet.

Sinking onto the side of the bed, she sucked in a sharp breath at the pain radiating down her shins. ''Ooh!''

Without asking for permission, the man shoved her skirt up to just above her knees. ''Damn! You're skinned up pretty bad, sweetpea.'' He reached over to a big red-and-black gym bag sitting on the end of the bed. ''Take off your panty hose.''

Before she could tell him she'd do no such thing,

there was a loud pounding on the door in the outer room. She jumped at the sound.

"Were you expecting someone?" she asked cautiously.

He looked through the doorway into the sitting area of the suite, then at her. "No." Grinning, he shrugged. "But I wasn't expecting you either."

"It's Patrick." Panic welled up inside her as she stood up and looked around the room. "He can't find me. I have to leave."

Brant Wakefield watched the woman desperately look for a way to escape the bedroom of his suite. She was as skittish as a pasture-raised colt. If he didn't reassure her, and damn quick, he had no doubt she'd be crawling back out onto that ledge.

"Hey, sweetpea, don't worry. I don't know who Patrick is, or why you're trying to get away from him, but I won't give you away." He walked to the door. "Sit tight. I'll get rid of whoever's out there, then we'll take care of bandaging those scrapes."

Pulling the bedroom door almost shut, Brant walked across the sitting area. As soon as he got rid of whoever was on the other side of the outer door, he intended to get some answers from his unexpected guest.

Another knock, this time harder, came from the other side. Brant squinted one eye and looked through the peephole. A man wearing a dark-gray, pin-striped suit stood with his fist raised to impatiently pound on the door again.

Aw, hell. The guy was a "suit." If there was one thing Brant despised, it was a "suit." You just couldn't trust them. And Brant would bet good money that the slick-looking suit on the other side of the door was the one the lady in his bedroom wanted to avoid.

Brant sized up his opponent. He was at least six inches taller and outweighed the guy by a good thirty pounds. And unless the little weasel held a black belt in martial arts, Brant could take him in a fight. Easy.

Sure his expression reflected his irritation, as well as his disdain, Brant released the locks and threw the door open wide. "What the hell do *you* want?" he demanded.

The suit took a step back. "I...uh, I'm sorry to disturb you, but I'm looking for my fiancée." He held a picture up for Brant's inspection. "I was wondering if you've seen her."

Brant didn't like lying. It was dishonest any way you looked at it. But he was well aware of his state of undress. It wouldn't be his fault if the guy assumed that Brant had been playing some kind of bedroom game with a willing little filly.

"The only woman I've seen lately is the one taking off her panty hose in the bedroom," he answered truthfully. He folded his arms across his bare chest and stared down at the man. "And I was right in the middle of helping her when *you* interrupted us."

The man's grin made Brant immediately drop his arms to his sides and clench his hands into tight fists. He'd like nothing more than the pleasure of wiping that lecherous smile off the man's pasty face with a good right hook.

Brant was once again reminded of why he disliked most of the suits of the world. They used their expensive clothes to hide their unscrupulous nature. But the guy standing before him was one, Brant knew for a fact, he'd despise no matter what kind of clothes he wore. He just had a shifty look about him that set Brant's teeth on edge and said louder than words that the guy was as crooked as a barrel of fishhooks.

"I'll let you get back to your evening's entertainment," the man said, pulling a card and an ink pen from the inside pocket of his suit coat. Scribbling on the back, he handed it to Brant. "Here's my name and room number. If you see a rather plain-looking woman wearing a khaki-colored skirt and an off-white blouse, give me a call."

Brant had to hold himself in check to keep from punching the guy right square in the nose. The woman might not be a beauty queen, but she deserved to be thought of by her fiancé as more than just "plain-looking." He turned the business card over in his hand and noticed that it read Patrick Elsworth, Esquire, Certified Public Accountant. Shrugging, Brant reached to close the door.

"She wears black, plastic-framed glasses," the man added as Brant slammed the door in his face.

Securing the locks, he walked over to the waste-basket by the desk and tossed the card inside, then pushed the door open to the bedroom. The woman was nowhere in sight.

"Lady?" Nothing. "Hey, lady?"

Where the hell could she have gone? Was she outside on the balcony? Or worse yet, walking the ledge around the building again?

His heart pounded at the thought. Although he didn't know the woman, he sure as hell didn't want to see anything happen to her. Just when he decided to check the balcony, the bathroom door opened a crack.

"Is he gone?" she whispered.

Brant nodded. ''We won't be hearing any more from him tonight.''

She opened the door wider and stood there looking uncertain. With her black-rimmed glasses and the dubious look in her green eyes, she reminded him of his first-grade teacher, Mrs. Andrews, when he'd tried to tell her that he hadn't meant to slip a grasshopper down the back of Susie Parker's dress—that it had jumped there all by itself.

''How do you know he won't be back?'' the woman asked, sounding as doubtful as she looked.

''Because I made it clear that I didn't appreciate being disturbed,'' Brant said. Grinning, he innocently splayed his hands and shrugged, hoping to put her at ease. ''I can't help it if he thinks I'm in here getting up close and personal with a buckle bunny.''

''What's that?'' She shook her head as she limped toward the door. ''Don't tell me. I think I have a pretty good idea already.''

Brant followed her into the sitting room. She'd taken her straight, pale-blond hair down from the twist at the back of her head and he was amazed at how much younger she looked. When he'd first seen her staring at him through the balcony door, he'd have judged her to be somewhere in her mid to late thirties. But now? Shoot, she couldn't be more than twenty-four or twenty-five years old.

He also noticed that she'd removed her torn panty hose. Swallowing hard, he tried to wipe the image of her trim calves and slender ankles from his obviously overtired brain by averting his gaze to her feet. It surprised him to see her toenails were painted with fire engine-red polish. It just seemed out of place, considering the rest of her attire was so—he refused to use the word *plain* to describe her—conservative. Yeah, that was the word. Conservative.

As she walked across the room, Brant decided it was none of his business what color the lady painted her toenails, or that she was hiding great-looking legs beneath that oversize skirt.

"Have a seat and take it easy while I go throw on some clothes." Focusing on the injuries he'd noticed when he first escorted her from the balcony into his bedroom, he added, "Then I'll take care of patching up your knees."

She nodded and sank down on the couch. Staring up at him for several seconds, she pushed her glasses up with a brush of her hand and cleared her throat. "I didn't mean to be nosy, but I couldn't help noticing that you have several jars of greasepaint on the counter in your bathroom. Are you some type of clown?" she asked politely.

"Not exactly." He almost laughed out loud. From the cautious tone of her voice, it sounded more like she was asking if he was some kind of crook who used greasepaint for his disguises. "I'm a bullfighter."

"A matador?" She looked doubtful again. "I didn't think they painted their faces."

"Wrong kind of bullfighting," he said, unable to keep his smile from breaking through. "I work rodeos and bull riding events. I'm in town this weekend with the PBR."

"What's that?"

"Professional Bull Riders."

"That's very…interesting, Mr.…." She paused, her cheeks coloring a pretty pink. "I'm so embarrassed.

You've gone out of your way to be kind to me and I don't even know your name.''

"Brant Wakefield.''

"I'm Anastasia Devereaux,'' she said, politely extending her hand.

"Glad to meet you, Miss Devereaux.'' He reached out to shake her hand, but the moment her soft palm touched his, a jolt of electric current zinged up his arm and exploded in his chest. He swallowed hard and, pulling his hand back, flexed his fingers. He must be getting a case of that carpal tunnel something or other that everyone was talking about having.

Incapable of speech, he turned and walked into the bedroom. He'd been getting ready to take a shower when she knocked on the balcony door, but that could wait until after he'd taken care of her scraped-up hands and knees. The way she'd limped when she crossed the sitting room, he'd bet her knees were getting sore as hell.

He tugged the knot of the towel loose at his waist, pulled on a pair of underwear, jeans and a T-shirt, then reached back into his heavy-duty canvas bag for the first-aid kit he took everywhere he went. Heading back into the sitting room, he stopped short at the sight of her huddled on the couch, her arms wrapped around her middle, shivering uncontrollably. A knot formed in his gut and he could have kicked himself in the rear for not offering her a blanket or his coat.

Pulling the coffee table out of the way, Brant knelt in front of her, set the first-aid kit on the carpet beside him, then rubbed his hands up and down her arms in an attempt to warm her. Unless he missed his guess, her reaction had more to do with walking along the ledge than with braving the freezing temperature outside.

"I'll get my jacket for you," he said, rising to his feet.

He went back into the bedroom, then returned to drape his heavy, leather-and-wool varsity-style jacket over her shoulders. As an afterthought, he lifted her hair from beneath the collar. The thick shoulder-length strands flowed over his hands like golden silk threads and he had to fight to keep from tangling his fingers in them.

"That should warm you up in no time," he said, taking a step back. It for damn sure raised his temperature several notches and had him wondering what the hell had gotten into him.

"Th-thank y-you," she said through chattering teeth.

Kneeling in front of her again, he lifted her skirt above her knees and tried not to notice the lovely expanse of smooth feminine thighs mere inches from his fingers. He took a deep breath, uncapped a small bottle of antiseptic and hoped the smell would clear his head.

"Would you like to tell me what this is all about?" he asked as he soaked a piece of gauze with the antiseptic, then dabbed it on her scraped skin.

"No," she said quickly. She hesitated for several seconds before she finally spoke again. "I'm sorry, but I don't think that would be a good idea."

Brant stopped tending her wounds to study her expression. He could tell she wasn't sure she should confide in him. All things considered, he could understand her hesitation. After all, she didn't know him or anything about his character.

"You can trust me," he said, looking directly into her wide green eyes. Eyes that if a man wasn't careful, he could get lost in. He suddenly had to clear his throat before he could speak. "I just want to help you out of whatever trouble you're in."

"What makes you think that I'm in trouble?" she asked, sounding defensive.

"Something drove you out onto that ledge." He turned his attention back to the abrasions on her knees. "And I'm betting it wasn't that you just wanted to get a breath of fresh air." He capped the small bottle of antiseptic and reached for a tube of antibacterial ointment. "Why don't you start by explaining why you're running from your fiancé?"

Her hand shook as she pushed her glasses up on her nose again. "I don't know you."

"That's true," he said, nodding. "But under the circumstances, I don't think you have a choice. It's clear you need help and since I don't see anyone else volunteering for the job, I'm your best bet." A sudden thought caused him to glance up at her. "Did the suit get rough with you?"

If he had, Brant had every intention of finding old pasty-faced Patrick and making him sorry he'd ever been born. No man abused a woman when Brant was around to put a stop to it. Bar none.

"Not exactly," she answered, shaking her head. "He was too busy threatening—" Snapping her mouth shut, she sat there staring at Brant for several long moments. "I...don't think it would be wise to involve you," she finally said, sounding tired.

"Why don't you tell me what's going on and let me make up my own mind?" He applied the salve to the scrapes on her knees as he waited for her to decide what to do. Just when he thought she was going to decline his offer, he heard her take a deep breath.

Glancing up, he caught her watching him. The apprehension in her big green eyes twisted his gut. Anastasia Devereaux was up against a wall and scared witless.

"You've been more than kind, Mr. Wakefield. But—"

"The name's Brant."

She nodded. "Patrick is running out of options. And desperate men resort to desperate measures. I don't want to involve you in my problems, Brant."

The sound of her soft voice saying his name did strange things to his insides and quickened his pulse. He concentrated on placing squares of gauze on her wounds and tried to ignore the feeling. He must have landed on his head earlier in the evening and just couldn't remember it. The lady in front of him wasn't his type. Not by a long shot.

Aside from the fact that the women he normally found attractive wore makeup and their clothes fit more snugly, Anastasia's demeanor and manners practically shouted culture and refined living. For that matter, so did her name. And although his bank account proved that he was quite successful at bullfighting, and his degree in ranch management attested to the fact that he was far from being a country bumpkin, he sure as hell wasn't the refined, academic type.

Besides, she was engaged to that slick little weasel, Patrick. And Brant wasn't one to tread on another man's territory, even if the guy wasn't good enough to breathe the same air she did.

"It would be best if I found a way to escape the hotel undetected and leave you out of this," she said, reminding Brant that whether she was his type of woman or not, the lady was in a heap of trouble and needed help.

"I can take care of myself," he said, unwrapping a roll of gauze. He wound it around her leg, then secured the bandage with tape. "And I give you my word that your fiancé will have to come through me before he lays a hand on you, Annie."

Anastasia sucked in a sharp breath. The only people who had ever defied her grandmother's decree that she be called anything but Anastasia had been her parents, Jack and Christine Devereaux. They'd called her Annie, and she'd forgotten how much she missed the informal shortening of her name.

A deep sadness knifed through her as she thought of her parents. Even though they had died nineteen years ago—just after her fifth birthday—she still remembered them and couldn't help but wonder how different her life would have been if they'd lived to raise her.

She took a deep, steadying breath to chase away her sense of loss. It was nonproductive to spend time dwelling on what might have been. Even if her grandmother had never allowed her to experience anything even remotely adventurous, she'd had a very nice childhood. Her grandmother said so. And whatever Carlotta Whittmeyer said, well, that's just the way it was. No one dared contradict one of her grandmother's edicts. Ever.

Turning her attention back to the man tending her wounds, Annie bit her lower lip. Brant Wakefield seemed trustworthy. And heaven only knew she could use a friend right now.

"I...don't know where to start," she said, not at

all certain she should be telling a stranger why she'd fled from the room next door and taken the uncharacteristic risk of walking along the narrow ledge surrounding the hotel. Or why it was imperative that she avoid Patrick Elsworth for the next week.

"Why don't you start at the beginning?" Brant asked, winking at her.

His smile was encouraging and her heart skipped a beat at the gesture. She refused to acknowledge it as anything but a case of nerves from the evening's harrowing events. She never had been, and never would be, the excitable type.

"Patrick is my grandmother's accountant," Annie said, choosing her words carefully.

"Is that how the two of you met?"

She shook her head. "No. He was a regular borrower at the library where I work. He'd been coming in for several weeks before he asked me to have dinner with him. That was a little over a year ago."

"So you've been seeing him for some time?" Brant asked, one eyebrow raised in question.

"Yes." Suddenly feeling as if all the strength had been drained from her body, Annie leaned her head against the back of the couch. "And before this goes any further, I think I should set the record straight. Patrick Elsworth never has been, nor will he ever be, my fiancé."

Two

Brant sat back on his heels to stare at the sparkling diamond on the third finger of Annie's left hand. "Then what's that?" he asked, pointing to the impressive ring. "Last time I heard, a rock like that is a man's way of branding a woman as his."

"It's the engagement ring Patrick *tried* to give me," she answered, as if that explained everything.

"This guy asked you to marry him, you took the ring, but you aren't engaged." Brant wanted to make sure he had things straight.

"Correct."

Brant turned his attention back to the first-aid kit as he pondered her explanation. Maybe it was logical to a woman, but it didn't make a damn bit of sense to him. Unless she...

He shot her a glance. The diamond had to be worth

several thousand dollars. Had she stolen the expensive piece of jewelry?

As if she'd read his mind, she shook her head. "Before you ask if I'm a thief, the answer is no. The ring rightfully belongs to my grandmother and I have every intention of seeing that she gets it."

Brant was more confused than ever. "You mean this guy was trying to give you an engagement ring that belongs to your grandmother, and you're wearing it, but you didn't accept it and you're not going to marry him."

"Exactly."

"Are you sure you started at the beginning?" he asked. "Either I've missed something, or you've left out a bunch of pretty important details."

She fidgeted with the hem of her skirt before she pulled it down over her bandaged knees, blocking his view of her shapely thighs. "I've been seeing Patrick socially for the past year—"

"I got that much," Brant said, rising to his feet. He pulled the coffee table back into place, then sat on it, putting himself directly in front of her. Reaching for her right hand, he began cleaning the abrasions on her palm. He tried to ignore the fact that her skin was possibly the softest he'd ever felt. "Why don't you fast-forward to the events that led up to your being in his hotel room and what drove you out onto a ten-inch ledge?" he asked to distract himself.

"We'd been seeing each other for a few months when Patrick started giving my grandmother tips on investments and tax shelters, even though she already had a very competent accountant," Annie explained.

Brant wrapped gauze around her hand. "Let me

guess. It wasn't long before she switched bean counters.''

She nodded. ''Correct. Grandmother dismissed Mr. Bennett, the CPA she'd had for years, to hire Patrick. At first, everything seemed fine. But then I started noticing a change in him.''

Brant replaced the contents of the first-aid kit. ''What was different?''

''It wasn't anything overly obvious, at first,'' she said, fingering the expensive engagement ring. ''Patrick started wearing nicer, more expensive clothing, and I thought he might have been put on retainer by a few more clients.'' She shook her head. ''But in the last couple of months he's replaced his economy car with a BMW, bought a new home in a prestigious subdivision and furnished it with pricey antiques and original art. I thought he might have gone into debt for all of it. Then he started bragging that he'd paid cash for everything but the house. That's when I realized something was seriously wrong. An accountant who opened his firm on a shoestring budget in a town the size of ours, couldn't possibly afford to do those things in less than a year's time.''

''You aren't from Saint Louis?''

''No. We live in Herrin, a small town southeast of here. Over in Illinois. The population is somewhere around ten thousand, so I'm certain he hasn't been making *that* kind of money.''

Common sense told Brant that it took a lot longer than a year to build a business to the level where it paid that well, even in a city. ''It does sound pretty suspicious,'' Brant admitted, snapping the lid shut on the medical kit.

''That's what I thought.'' She continued to twist

the diamond ring around the third finger of her left hand. "But until this evening, that was all I had—suspicions."

Brant jerked his head up to look at her. "So now you have proof?"

She nibbled her lower lip before she finally answered. "Not exactly."

"Then how can you be sure he's been stealing money from your grandmother?" Getting her to give him all the details was like pulling teeth.

She suddenly stood to pace the room. As he watched her, he found the sight of his big jacket dwarfing her small frame oddly endearing. He sucked in a sharp breath. Where the hell had that come from?

Now he knew for certain that he must have landed on his head sometime during the first round of the bull riding event. He reached up and ran a hand over his scalp. But there weren't any lumps or tender places…

"I know Patrick has been embezzling from Grandmother because he admitted it this evening just before he asked me to marry him," Annie said as she walked the perimeter of the sitting room.

"You mean this jerk admitted to stealing from your grandmother, then wanted you to marry him?" Brant asked incredulously.

"Yes."

He shook his head. "I'll give the little weasel this much, he's got a set of solid-brass balls."

She stopped pacing to look at him. "That's exactly what I thought. But when I told Patrick that I'd rather die than marry him—" She closed her eyes and shuddered. "He said that could easily be arranged."

Brant was on his feet and standing in front of her in a split second. "The guy threatened your life?"

"Yes."

"Do you think he meant it?"

She nodded. "Yes, I believe so." Nervously adjusting her glasses, she sighed. "In fact, I know he did. He's just that desperate."

Brant's gut burned with anger and he found himself regretting that he hadn't buried his fist in the suit's face when he'd had the opportunity. Placing his hands on her shoulders, Brant tried to ignore the current that seemed to radiate from her body to his as he stared down at her. "You have to call the police, Annie."

"And tell them what?" she asked, her green eyes shadowed with doubts. "Even though Patrick admitted to stealing money from my grandmother and threatened me, I have no proof and no witnesses. And we both know if the authorities inquired about either incident, he would deny everything." She shook her head. "They couldn't do anything, because it would be a case of he said, she said—his word against mine."

Mulling over what she'd said, Brant had to admit that Annie was probably right. The police couldn't do anything without some type of solid evidence.

"If you suspected him of being that big of a snake, what were you doing in his room?"

"I've asked myself that same question about a thousand times since dinner," she said, sounding disgusted. "All I can come up with is naiveté or sheer stupidity. And at this point, I'm leaning toward the latter."

"You're being too hard on yourself, Annie," Brant

said, slipping his hands beneath the jacket to massage the tension he felt in her slender shoulders.

"I should have known better." She shrugged. "But Grandmother has a couple of accounts in the banks up here, and when Patrick told me he had a business meeting in Saint Louis with one of the bankers, and asked me to come along, I thought I might have the opportunity to find something to incriminate him."

"I take it you didn't find anything?" Even though her silk blouse lay between his palms and her satiny skin, Brant enjoyed the feel of her softness beneath his hands.

"No, I didn't find out anything because there was never a meeting scheduled." Closing her eyes, she shook her head. "It was nothing more than a ploy to get me to accompany him to this hotel and get me to take a trip down the aisle. He said that he'd known I was getting suspicious and that it was just a matter of time before I told my grandmother. So he bought this ring with more of my grandmother's money and here I am."

Brant stopped rubbing her shoulders. Now he was really confused. "How would the two of you getting married solve anything? You could still tell your grandmother and she could have him arrested."

Annie opened her eyes and shook her head ruefully. "Patrick knows how Grandmother is. She would never file charges against her only granddaughter's husband, no matter what he'd done. It would create too much of a scandal." She shook her head. "And anything that casts a bad light on the Whittmeyer family is to be avoided at all costs."

Brant detected a bitter undertone to her quietly spoken explanation. Anger twisted his gut to think that her grandmother would sacrifice Annie and her happiness for the sake of the family name. Stepping away from her, he stuffed his hands in the hip pockets of his jeans before he did something stupid like pull her into his arms to offer her comfort. The trouble was, he wasn't sure comfort was all he wanted to offer. Which, all things considered, was ridiculous. He'd known the woman less than an hour.

"Why not call your grandmother, fill her in on what you know and let her get an auditor to go over her accounts?" he asked, wondering why his voice suddenly sounded like a rusty hinge. He cleared his throat. "Or maybe she can just fire this character and chalk all of it up to experience."

Annie's soft sigh sent a streak of protectiveness straight through him. "I can't. Grandmother is on a tour of European museums and won't return for another week." She walked over to sink down on the couch. "And to tell you the truth, I'm not even sure which country she's in right now."

"Is there anyone else you could get hold of?" Brant asked. "What about your parents? Or maybe an aunt or uncle?"

Annie shook her head. "My parents died nineteen years ago. All Grandmother and I have are each other." She pulled his coat more closely around her. "Walking that ledge wasn't the smartest thing I've ever done, but it was all I could think of. I wasn't about to marry Patrick, and I have to stay alive until Grandmother returns so I can explain what's going on."

Annie looked so small and lonely sitting there in his big coat that it was all Brant could do to keep from sitting down beside her and pulling her into his arms. Instead, he ran a hand across the back of his neck and tried to get his mind off the way she looked and return to the business at hand.

"How did you manage to get away from him long enough to crawl out there and make it over to my balcony?" Brant finally asked, deciding it was best to let her do the talking. Otherwise, he might end up acting on his first impulse.

"Patrick had gone into the sitting area of his suite to make phone calls to reserve a chapel in Las Vegas and make airline reservations. That's when I grabbed the ring and escaped." She shuddered and Brant figured she was remembering how scary it had been out on that ledge. "Now all I have to do is find some tangible proof of my suspicions and figure out a way to avoid him for the next week," she said, looking tired.

"Going home is out of the question," Brant guessed, thinking out loud. "I'm betting that's the first place he'll look for you."

She nodded. "Hiding out in Herrin would be next to impossible. Everyone in town knows me." Taking her glasses off, she rubbed the bridge of her nose with thumb and forefinger. "But I really have nowhere else to go and no money to get there. I left my purse in Patrick's suite, along with my coat."

Brant had to concentrate hard on what she was saying. Without her glasses, she looked completely different. And although she wouldn't be considered pretty by conventional standards, she was *very* attractive.

"Don't worry about where you'll go or the money to get you there. I'll take you with me," he blurted out before he could stop himself.

Time seemed to come to a complete halt as they stared at each other. But the more Brant thought about the idea, the more it made sense. He might have met Annie Devereaux only an hour ago, and they might come from completely different walks of life, but it just wasn't in him to leave a woman to fend for herself when she was in trouble. No siree. He could no more walk away and leave her alone to deal with her problems than he could stop the sun from rising in the east every morning.

"I truly appreciate the offer, Brant. But I can't involve you any more than you already are," Annie said, standing to remove his coat. She handed the leather-sleeved jacket to him. "I'll find a way—"

"Too late, sweetpea," Brant interrupted. Smiling, he hooked his thumb over his shoulder toward the bedroom. "I got involved the minute you knocked on my balcony door."

"But—"

"But nothing. I have the way." He chuckled. "And believe me, I have more than enough means to get you out of here and keep you safe until your grandmother returns from her trip. And that's just what I'm going to do."

Annie blinked as she tried to comprehend what Brant was saying. "Stay with you? For a week?"

"Yep."

"I can't do that."

"Why not?"

"Because…because…I just can't," she stammered. "I don't know you or anything about you."

He nodded. "I understand that. But we can remedy that right now."

As she stared at him, Annie couldn't seem to focus

on anything but how handsome he was and what a nice smile he had. Brant Wakefield was—as Tiffany, her teenage assistant at the library, would say—really hot. His eyes were quite possibly the bluest she'd ever seen and radiated an integrity that she'd never seen in Patrick's pale-gray gaze.

But that was only the beginning of Brant's rugged appeal. The sound of his sexy baritone would take the breath of every female who still had a pulse. And his touch was…magic. That's the only word she could think of that even remotely described how it had felt when he'd cleaned and bandaged her skinned knees and hand. His fingers brushing her leg as he tended the scrapes had sent tingling sensations straight up her thigh to the most feminine part of her. The fact that he had a body to die for didn't hurt her impression of him either.

"What would you like to know about me?" Brant asked, interrupting her introspection as he placed his coat back around her shoulders.

Annie sucked in a sharp breath at his nearness and the mingled scents of spicy cologne, leather and man swirling around her. Brant Wakefield was too male, and much too close for her peace of mind.

She sank back down on the couch in order to put distance between them. "What was the question?"

He once again seated himself on the coffee table directly in front of her. Resting his forearms on his knees, he patiently repeated his question. "What would you like to know about me?"

How your lips would feel as you kissed me? How your body would feel pressed to mine if we…?

Annie gulped and glanced down at her tightly twisted hands, resting in her lap. What on earth had gotten into her? She wasn't in the habit of fantasizing about men she dated, let alone a total stranger. Which Brant was.

"I…uh, what do you want me to know?" she finally managed to ask.

His smile was so darned charming that her stomach fluttered wildly. "Let's see. You already know my name and that I'm a bullfighter in town with the PBR." He paused for a moment. "I'm thirty-two, I own the Lonetree Ranch in central Wyoming with my brothers, Morgan and Colt. And when I get too old to dodge bulls for a living, I intend to raise bucking horses for rodeo. Anything else you'd like to know?"

Her gaze flew to his left hand. He didn't wear a wedding band, but that didn't mean he wasn't committed to a relationship. "Won't your girlfriend object to my being with you for the next week?"

"I don't have one."

"Oh."

He grinned. "Now, don't go getting the wrong impression there, sweetpea. I like women. A lot. I just haven't found the right one yet."

"I never thought…" Heat flooded her cheeks. Anything she said would end up embarrassing her more. Deciding to change the direction of the conversation, she asked, "But how would you get me out of the hotel without Patrick seeing us?"

"Leave that to me," Brant said, rising to his feet. He walked over to the phone on the desk and picked up the receiver.

Annie couldn't believe she was actually contemplating going along with his crazy scheme. But as she watched him punch in a phone number, she realized that as scary as the idea was of spending the next week with the most handsome cowboy—make that the only cowboy—she'd ever met, it was also oddly exhilarating.

"Hey, Sarah. It's Brant. I need your help with something," he said into the phone. He paused. "Yeah, I know what time it is." Grinning, he held the receiver away from his ear and winked at Annie. "Sarah's the on-site event coordinator. She's just a little bent out of shape right now over my waking her up at one-thirty in the morning."

"Maybe this wasn't such a good idea," Annie said, hearing the woman's raised voice all the way across the room.

He chuckled. "She'll get over it." Placing the receiver back to his ear, he nodded. "Yeah, I know you'll get even. Now jot this down. I need you to pick up a woman's hat, shirt and jeans in size…" He turned back to Annie. "What size do you wear?"

"Ten, but—"

"Shoe size?"

"Seven."

"Make the shirt and jeans a size eight, a pair of boots in a ladies' size seven and a hat that would fit you." He listened a moment, then laughed. "Yeah, I know I owe you, Sarah. Just charge everything to my room and have it here first thing in the morning. Oh, we'll also need a PBR varsity jacket in small added to that order."

As soon as he hung up the phone, Annie shook her head. "I can't wear a size eight or anything in a small size. They'll be too tight."

His charming grin made her lower stomach do that strange little fluttering thing again. "Trust me, sweet-pea. They'll fit just fine."

* * *

The next morning Brant checked his watch for the fifth time in as many minutes. As soon as Sarah dropped off the things he'd asked her to buy, Annie had spoken to the woman privately, then waited for Sarah to return with some undisclosed item, grabbed the packages of clothes and disappeared through the bedroom door. That had been a good half hour ago and he hadn't seen her since.

Just when he decided she'd probably drowned in the shower, or crawled back out onto the ledge to escape him the way she had the crooked little bean counter, Brant heard the bedroom door open. Spinning around, he opened his mouth to ask what had taken so long, but the sight of the woman standing uncertainly in the doorway brought him up short.

He grinned. "Damn, sweetpea. You clean up real nice."

She gave him a doubtful look over the top of her glasses. "I'm not too sure about this."

"What's wrong?" He didn't see a single thing wrong with the way she looked. Far from it. In the figure category Annie Devereaux was about as perfect as a woman could get.

"These jeans may be made of stretch denim, but they're still a lot tighter than I'm used to," she protested. "And the blouse is a bit too snug."

When she twisted to look at her behind in the mirror above the desk, the fabric of the red and blue western-cut blouse pulled tight over her breasts, causing Brant's mouth to go bone dry. The shirt was snug all right, but in a good way. A damn good way.

Turning, she bent over to pick up a tag that she'd dropped on the carpet. His heart stopped, then took off at a gallop. Did she have anything on under those jeans? He'd seen more women in stretch jeans than he could count and they'd all had a little ridge where their panties went around their legs. But Annie didn't have any kind of detectable line to indicate that she did or didn't have on underwear. The thought that she might not have on anything inside those jeans sent his blood pressure up several notches.

Averting his eyes to the top of her blond head, he cleared the rust from his throat. "The clothes are perfect. You'll blend in with the crowd and Elsworth won't recognize you if he walks right by you."

She nibbled at her lower lip. "I suppose that's what we want, isn't it?"

Brant nodded. "That's exactly what we want, sweetpea. It's your ticket out of here."

"I guess you're right." Lifting her long hair and twisting it as if to put it up in a bun, she shrugged. "Once we get out of the hotel, I'll find somewhere to change back into my skirt and blouse."

"Not unless you want to stick out like a sore thumb," he said bluntly. He adjusted his black Resistol, then picked up the matching one Sarah had bought for Annie. Handing it to her, he said, "Leave your hair down and put this on."

She stared at the wide-brimmed hat in her hands. "I've never worn anything like this."

"All the more reason to put it on." He took the hat from her and positioned it on top of her head. "Elsworth won't be looking for a shapely blond in jeans, boots and a black Resistol. He's going to have his eye out for a little wren in baggy clothes."

"A what?"

Brant chuckled. "In that oversize tan skirt and off-white blouse you looked like a frightened little wren.''

"I did not.''

"Did too.''

"My clothes are not baggy,'' she said defensively. "They're just not formfitting. And neutral colors are quite fashionable.''

He snorted. "If you're trying to look like a wren.'' Stepping back, he allowed his gaze to travel from the top of her hat to her new boots. He frowned. "Can you see without your glasses?''

"Not well.'' She pushed the black frames up with a brush of her hand. "I'm nearsighted and things at a distance are kind of fuzzy.''

"But you won't walk into a wall or anything like that if you take them off?''

"No.''

"Then let me have them,'' he said, extending his hand. "I'll put them in my shirt pocket and give them back once we're out of here and on the way to the arena.''

Annie dutifully removed her glasses and handed them to him. "I've thought about getting contacts, but I've worn glasses so long, I'm not sure how I would look without them.''

He grinned. "Trust me, sweetpea. You'd look just fine.''

Was that appreciation she detected in Brant's eyes? The kind of look a man had when he found a woman attractive?

Her heart skipped a beat, but she quickly abandoned the silly notion. Whether she wore glasses or not, she never had been, nor would she ever be, the type of woman that men noticed for longer than it took to acknowledge her presence, then dismiss her.

She watched Brant move around the room as he packed the rest of his things in the big red-and-black duffel bag. The glint she thought she'd seen in his deep blue gaze was probably nothing more than an illusion due to her blurred vision from not wearing her glasses.

"Get the clothes you had on before you changed," he said as he scooped up a handful of coins and his wallet from the desktop. "When we leave the Savvis Center this evening, we'll go straight to the airport."

When she retrieved her skirt and blouse, with her underthings hidden safely within the folds, he stuffed them into the bag and zipped it shut. The sight activated the butterflies in her stomach. There was something oddly intimate about having her clothes packed with his in the duffel bag.

"Are you ready to go?" he asked, holding the varsity jacket he'd had the event coordinator bring along with the other clothes for her. Thankfully the woman had been understanding when Annie requested she make another trip to the store for the change of underwear that Annie had been too embarrassed to request the night before, and that Brant hadn't thought of.

"Not really," she said, unable to stop a nervous giggle from escaping as she slipped her arms into the waist-length coat with the PBR logo on the back. "What time does the bull riding start?"

"In a couple of hours." He shrugged into his own jacket, then picked up the duffel bag and guided her toward the door. "But we need to catch a ride to the Savvis Center and grab a bite to eat in the VIP lounge before I have to get my clothes changed and my face on.''

''Your face?''

He laughed as he released the locks and opened the door. ''The greasepaint.''

Annie had to force her boot-clad feet to step out of the safety of Brant's room and into the hall. To her relief, there were no other hotel guests in the corridor.

She must have looked as apprehensive as she felt, because Brant reached down and took her hand in his as they walked to the elevator. ''Hang in there, Annie,'' he said quietly. ''Everything is going to be all right.''

His warm palm securely holding hers was reassuring and she found herself beginning to believe that his crazy scheme just might work. ''Brant, I really appreciate everything you've done for—''

But before she could finish thanking him, he suddenly dropped the duffel bag and tugged her into his arms. Reaching up, he pushed the brim of his hat up, then did the same to hers.

''What do you think you're—''

''Hush, sweetpea,'' he said a moment before his firm lips covered hers in a kiss that made her knees wobble and curled her toes inside her brand-new boots.

Three

As Brant brought his mouth down on Annie's, he tried to keep an eye on the man he'd seen step off the elevator. Patrick Elsworth was walking right toward them and Brant wanted to make sure he kept her turned so that she wouldn't be recognized.

But the feel of her soft lips beneath his and the slight weight of her pressed against him sent Brant's blood pressure up close to stroke range and made concentrating on anything but the woman in his arms damn near impossible. He tightened his hold to draw her more fully against him and her lips parted on a small gasp. He couldn't have stopped himself from deepening the kiss if his life depended on it.

The silkiness of her straight blond hair flowing over his hands, the sweet taste of her as her tongue timidly met his, had him forgetting all about the man approaching them. Annie kissed like a shy angel, but her full breasts pressed to his chest reminded him that she was a flesh-and-blood woman with a body made for a man's loving. Brant's lower body responded in a way that totally agreed with the thought.

"Good morning," Elsworth said, stopping beside them.

Brant broke the kiss and nodded a silent greeting, but continued to hold Annie close for several reasons. First of all, he was afraid she might panic and turn so that the man recognized her. Second, if he didn't hold on to her, Brant wasn't sure he could keep himself from hauling off and knocking the cocky little weasel into the middle of next week. But the biggest, most distracting reason he continued to hold her was far simpler than the first two. She just felt too damn good to let go.

When Elsworth failed to move on past them, Brant raised an eyebrow. "Was there something you wanted?"

The man nodded. "I'm still looking for my fiancée. I don't suppose either one of you have seen her this morning, have you?"

Brant felt Annie's body stiffen at the man's reference to their "engagement." Shaking his head, Brant tightened his arms around her and lowered his head to nuzzle the side of her neck. "Like I told you last night, the only woman I've seen is the one I'm holding right now."

Brant watched the man's gaze rake Annie's backside, lingering on her shapely behind and long slender legs encased in the snug denim. A fierce protectiveness surged through Brant and he possessively slid his hand down to her bottom in order to block the man's view. When he looked back up, Elsworth wore the same lascivious expression that had set Brant's teeth on edge the night before, and had him wanting to wipe off with his fist this morning.

"No wonder you didn't have time to discuss the matter with me last night," Elsworth said, winking at Brant.

"And I don't intend to talk to you about it now," Brant said, cutting off anything else the man could say.

He concentrated on kissing the hollow behind Annie's ear in order to hide the intense reaction he was sure colored his own expression. Patrick Elsworth's bold perusal of Annie's body had pure fury burning at Brant's gut. Which was ridiculous, considering that he was only trying to help her get out of the hotel undetected.

When he was sure he had control of the anger roiling inside him, Brant raised his head to give Elsworth a pointed look. "If you can't hold on to your woman, leave the ones of us who can alone."

To his immense satisfaction, Elsworth's irritating grin disappeared immediately and without another word he continued down the hall.

"Is he gone?" Annie whispered when Brant kept on holding her.

"I think so," he answered.

He tried to tell himself that the reason he held her close, still cupping her cute little rear in his hand, was in case Elsworth returned. But the truth of the matter was, he liked the way she felt against him and he wouldn't have minded picking up where he'd left off with the kiss.

The thought brought him up short. What the hell was he thinking? He'd kissed her for one reason and one reason only. To hide her identity from Elsworth. Nothing more.

Releasing her, Brant reached down to pick up his duffel bag, then ushered her to the elevator. "Let's get out of here before the jerk decides to come back," he said, feeling as if his jeans were a couple of sizes too tight in the stride.

Annie followed Brant to the elevator on wobbly legs. Having him hold her to his hard frame, feeling his large hand caress her bottom, had not only startled her to the point of speechlessness, it had unleashed a riot of sensations unlike any she'd ever known. When he took her into his arms, her heart had started racing and her breathing came out in short little puffs. That had been enough to scare her silly, but it was his kiss that made the world feel as if it came to a complete halt. She'd never been kissed like that in all of her twenty-four years.

His firm lips moving over hers had made her head spin, her knees rubbery and her insides flutter. But when his strong tongue dipped inside her mouth to explore, tease and taste, her body had started to tingle in places that had no business tingling. Most disturbing of all, the sensation hadn't stopped yet. And she refused to even begin to think about what the feel of his hand on her bottom had done to her newly awakened libido.

"Ready to catch a cab to the Savvis Center?" Brant asked, slipping a folded piece of paper into the inside pocket of his coat.

Annie looked around. When had they exited the elevator and walked over to the registration desk?

She'd been so lost in thought that she'd completely missed Brant checking out of the hotel.

What was wrong with her? She'd never been this easily distracted before. But with her insides quivering like a bowl of Jell-O and her heart skipping every other beat, she supposed it was understandable. What she couldn't comprehend was why she felt more alive than she had in her entire life.

"Are you all right, sweetpea?" Brant asked, looking concerned. He placed his hand at her back to guide her to the double doors leading outside.

"Uh…yes," she finally managed to say, forcing her legs to propel her forward. "I'm ready to leave whenever you are."

"Hey, Brant, wait up," a male voice called to them as they started through the hotel exit. "I want to talk to you about my draw."

She turned to watch a cowboy hurrying across the lobby toward them. "His draw?"

"The bull he's supposed to ride," Brant explained. He shook his head and swore softly. "This is the last thing I wanted to have happen." By the time the man walked up to them, Brant's easy expression had turned to a dark scowl. "I thought you were advised last night not to ride this afternoon."

"It was only a mild concussion," the man said, grinning. "Doc just cleared me to ride." He glanced at Annie, then seemed to do a double take as his gaze veered back, his grin widening. "Who's this lovely lady?"

Annie barely managed to stifle a surprised squeak when Brant slipped his arm around her waist and pulled her firmly against his side. "This is Annie. She's with me."

"Nice to meet you, Annie. I'm Colt Wakefield, this big galoot's younger, better-looking brother."

He extended his hand and even before he'd spoken the obvious, she could tell that Brant and Colt were related. Both had the same dark hair, the same startling blue eyes.

She heard Brant mutter an oath under his breath as she placed her hand in Colt's. "It's nice to meet you, Colt," she said. Was it her imagination, or had Brant tightened his arm around her waist?

"The pleasure's all mine, Annie," Colt said, enveloping her palm in his much larger one.

Colt Wakefield was every bit as good-looking as his older brother. But curiously, she felt none of the tingling sensations from his touch that she experienced from Brant's.

"We were just leaving for the Savvis Center," Brant said, his voice sounding more like a growl than his usual warm baritone.

"I'll ride along and you can tell me what you know about Black Magic," Colt said, following them through the double doors and out into the cold.

As they stood waiting for a cab, Brant held her close, using his big body to shield her from the sharp wind. Despite the bright noon sunshine, the temperature couldn't have been much above freezing. But surprisingly, she found that she was quite warm in the circle of Brant's strong arm.

"Turn out, little brother," Brant said, his tone more of a command than one of advice.

"You know I can't do that, bro," Colt said, shaking his head. "A turn out won't get me any closer to the finals at the end of the season."

"What's a turn out?" Annie asked.

A cab pulled to a stop in front of them and Brant opened the back passenger-side door and motioned for her to get in. He seated himself beside her before he answered, "A turn out is when a rider decides not to ride the bull he's drawn."

Colt slid into the back seat from the other side. "Yeah, Brant wants me to stand behind the chute while the gate opens and Black Magic walks out into the arena without me on his back." He snorted. "No way in hell I'm going to let that happen."

"Look, little brother, this is Black Magic's first season," Brant said, his expression grim. "He's young and unpredictable. You suffered a concussion during last night's round, and the last thing you need is to have your brains scrambled two days in a row."

Annie looked from one man to the other. Both of them wore the same stubborn expressions, had the same defiant tilt to their chins.

"I can't make the finals if I turn out," Colt said, glaring at his brother over the top of her head.

She watched a muscle work along Brant's lean jaw. "October is a long way off," he argued. "You can make up the points between now and then."

"I missed getting to go to the finals last year after Fireball mashed me against the gate and broke my ankle coming out of the chute in Detroit," Colt said stubbornly. "I'm not going to miss out this year because I don't have enough points." When the cab pulled to a stop at the back entrance of the arena, he threw open the door and got out. "Get used to it, big brother, I'm not turning out."

Brant exited on the opposite side, then extended his hand to help her as he continued to argue with his brother. "Dammit, Colt, you—"

"I'll do my job and make the ride," Colt interrupted, slamming the cab's door. "You just be there to do your job when it's time for me to dismount." Turning his attention to Annie, he touched the brim of his black cowboy hat with one finger. "It was nice meeting you, Annie. I hope to see you again sometime."

Before Annie could respond in kind, Colt's angry strides quickly carried him the distance to a door marked Personnel Only. Pulling it open, he disappeared inside the building without a backward glance.

"Damn fool," Brant muttered. "I swear he's twenty-six going on sixteen."

Annie glanced over at him. "Why don't you want your brother to ride this afternoon?"

His expression grim, he paid the cabdriver, then placed his hand at the small of her back to guide her through the same entrance Colt had used only moments before. "Colt's had three concussions in less than two months. If he doesn't start landing on his feet instead of his head, he's not going to have any brains left."

She remained silent as Brant showed his pass to the security guard. She'd never had siblings and had no idea what it would be like to feel so much concern for their well-being.

Brant led her down a long hall into a huge staging area, and looking around, Annie noticed a wide corridor to her left with signs indicating the training and press rooms were located somewhere beyond. To her right, several of the largest, most intimidating beasts she'd ever seen stood docilely inside a labyrinth of portable pens.

"Could I please have my glasses?" she asked,

wanting to get a better look. When Brant handed them to her, she put them on and stared openmouthed. "Are those the bulls Colt rides, and you fight?" she asked, shuddering at the sheer size of the animals.

He smiled. "Yep. Those are the best bucking bulls in the world."

She stared for several long seconds at the bulls, then at the handsome cowboy grinning at her. "You and Colt are both out of your minds. Just how many concussions have you suffered lately?"

After they had helped themselves to the buffet tables provided for the riders, contract personnel and their guests in the VIP lounge upstairs, Brant had taken her to a section of seats reserved for family and guests of the PBR, then left to change into his bull-fighting outfit. Sitting by herself as she stared out at the huge arena, Annie began to wonder if she wasn't the one who had lost her mind. She'd never before been the impulsive, adventurous type. But in the last fourteen hours, she'd done things she'd never in a million years have dreamed of doing—things that she hoped her grandmother never learned about.

She shook her head. If Carlotta Whittmeyer ever found out that Annie had walked along a hotel's narrow outside ledge several stories above an alley, and spent the night in a hotel suite with a man she didn't even know, Annie would never hear the end of it.

But she really couldn't fault the woman's need to squelch any adventurous streak Annie might have inherited from her parents. Her grandmother had good reason for being overly protective. She'd been faced with a parent's worst nightmare. Carlotta had lost her only daughter—her only child—when Annie's mother and father had been killed.

From the moment they met in college, until their untimely deaths eight years later, Christine and Jack Devereaux lived by the adage that life was meant to be experienced, not simply observed from the sidelines. They'd loved climbing mountains, exploring caves and navigating the rapids of the swiftest rivers. And when they weren't off in some remote part of the world pursuing their passion for extreme sports, they were planning their next trip. They'd even taken her with them occasionally, instead of leaving her with the nanny.

Had they lived, they might have instilled the same passion for adventure in their daughter. But a whitewater rafting accident had claimed their lives when Annie was five. That's when she'd gone to live with her grandmother.

Annie could remember as if it was yesterday how confused she'd been and how apprehensive she'd felt about going to live with a grandmother she barely knew. They'd both been suffering from the terrible loss and should have turned to each other for love and reassurance to see them through the difficult days following the accident. But instead of reaching out to comfort a frightened little girl who couldn't understand why she'd never see her beloved parents again, Carlotta had begun lecturing her on the foolishness of taking risks. That had been nineteen years ago and her grandmother hadn't missed a day since, cautioning Annie about placing herself in unnecessary danger, of the high price that being reckless and impulsive could cost.

Annie sighed. She was pretty sure her grandmother

loved her and had dealt with the situation the only way she'd known how. But Annie couldn't help feeling that their relationship could have—should have—been so much different.

"Do you mind if I join you?" a female voice asked, bringing her back to the present.

Glancing up, Annie saw a pretty, auburn-haired girl of about twenty standing next to her. "I don't mind at all," she said, smiling. "I'd like the company."

"I'm Kaylee Simpson," the girl said, sinking into the seat next to her.

"It's nice to meet you, Kaylee. I'm Ana…Annie."

The lights suddenly went out, ending the introduction, and a single spotlight came on, drawing attention to a cowboy standing in the center of the dirt-covered floor below. He identified himself as the president of the Professional Bull Riders, welcomed the crowd to the final two rounds of the Saint Louis Open and wished everyone an enjoyable afternoon.

When he finished, Kaylee leaned over to ask, "Are you here with someone?"

"Sort of," Annie said evasively.

She was saved any further comment when a loud boom signaled the beginning of a very impressive indoor pyrotechnics and laser display. Annie and Kaylee rose to their feet with the rest of the crowd when the theme from *Mission Impossible* blared from the loudspeakers, and giant sparklers ignited twin flames. The two trails of fire crawled across the dirt floor to the center of the arena, forming a lane that each cowboy riding in the event walked between as he was introduced to the cheering fans.

When Brant's brother Colt was introduced, Kaylee placed two fingers to her lips and let loose with an enthusiastic, ear-splitting whistle. "There's the man I'm going to marry," she said, her smile radiant.

As the opening ceremony ended, they sat back down and Annie watched the staging crew extinguish what was left of the fiery lane on the floor below. "How long have you been engaged to Colt, Kaylee?"

"Oh, we're not engaged," the girl answered, shaking her head. "Colt Wakefield barely knows I'm alive. He thinks I'm a kid."

"But I thought you said—"

"I will marry him," Kaylee said, nodding. "Just as soon as he wakes up and sees me as more than his best friend's baby sister."

When curiosity got the better of her, Annie asked, "How old are you?"

"I'll be twenty next month," Kaylee answered with a smile.

The announcer chose that moment to introduce the bullfighters, and at the mention of Brant's name, Annie's pulse quickened and she had to take a deep breath to steady her breathing. But the figure jogging out to the center of the floor looked nothing like Brant. Aside from the fact that he had bright pink, blue and yellow greasepaint stripes circling his mouth and eyes, the man's cowboy hat was battered and worn-looking, he wore a gaudy-colored long-sleeved shirt and a huge pair of cutoff jeans that looked like a ragged, denim miniskirt. Suspenders held the garment in place, and when he turned around she noticed that bandannas hung like limp flags from the back of the waistband, and large bright patches, advertising western products, covered the seat. Beneath the outlandish garb, it appeared that he wore bicycle shorts.

Thick pads covered both knees, and instead of cowboy boots, he wore athletic cleats.

"That's Colt's brother," Kaylee said.

"Brant," Annie agreed absently.

"You know him?"

"Sort of."

Kaylee laughed. "You sort of came with someone and you sort of know Brant." Her face lit with understanding. "Oh my God! Brant's the one you're with."

"No. Yes." Annie's cheeks burned. "It's complicated."

"I don't think I've ever known Brant to bring a date to one of the events before," Kaylee said thoughtfully.

"It's not like that." Annie watched Brant take his place beside a row of gates at the end of the arena. "We're just...just—"

What were they? Friends?

No. She and Brant really didn't even know each other. "We're...acquainted," she finally said, deciding that was the best definition of their unusual alliance.

Clearly not buying the explanation, Kaylee laughed. "If you say so." The girl's expression suddenly changed to one of concern. "You won't say anything to Brant, will you? You know, about my wanting to marry Colt?"

Smiling, Annie shook her head. "Your secret's safe with me."

"Thanks." Looking relieved, the girl shrugged one shoulder. "I don't want my brother, or Colt, finding out how I feel about him. They'd tease me something awful and never let me hear the end of it."

Their attention was suddenly drawn back to the arena floor with the announcement of the first bull rider.

"There's my man," Kaylee said proudly. "Right now, Colt's in fifth place in the point standings. But my brother, Mitch, is breathing down his neck. Mitch is only two places behind Colt."

Two men—one holding the end of a long rope attached to a gate, the other appearing to hold the closure shut—stood at one end of the arena. The man holding the metal gate suddenly let go, while the other man jerked hard on the rope. Both quickly stepped back as it swung wide and a black bull with Colt on its back exploded from the chute.

As if asking for divine intervention, Colt held one arm above his head, while his other arm extended down between his legs, where his hand appeared to be tied to the animal's broad back. Fascinated, Annie watched the large beast jump, spin and twist in an effort to dislodge Colt. She wondered how on earth he would manage to get loose and make it to safety without being seriously injured.

It didn't take long to find out, when the sound of a horn blew and Colt reached down with the hand he'd been holding above his head to pull on the rope, freeing himself from the bull. As the angry animal continued to buck wildly, Colt jumped from its back and ran for the fence surrounding the arena floor. But instead of the beast ignoring the man running from it, as Annie had hoped would be the case, the bull gave chase.

Annie blew out her pent-up breath when it appeared that Colt would win the footrace to safety. But her relief was short-lived. He suddenly stumbled and fell to his knees. The bull, seeing the object of its fury at a disadvantage, bore down on Colt with its sharp-looking horns lowered to do serious damage.

Annie's heart pounded wildly against her rib cage and fear streaked up her spine as she helplessly watched the horrifying scene playing out before her. But what happened next made her heart stop completely.

The bandannas tied to the back of his costume flapping wildly, Brant jumped in front of the bull and slapped it on the end of the nose. To Annie's horror the bull turned, and with a loud bellow lowered its deadly-looking horns to chase him.

Four

Time stood still as Annie watched the large, black bull charge Brant, while Colt made it to the safety of the fence. Dodging to one side, then the other, Brant stayed one step ahead of the angry animal as it relentlessly pursued him across the arena.

Then just as quickly as the chase began, it was over. Brant had maneuvered the bull back toward the bucking chutes where a gate had been thrown wide. Obviously seeing a way to escape the noise and bright lights, the beast lost interest in Brant and trotted docilely through the opening and out of sight. One of the cowboys standing close by shut the gate, and the wildly cheering crowd turned their attention to the replay of Colt's ride on the huge four-sided screen hanging high above the arena.

Annie released her pent-up breath and tried to concentrate on slowing the erratic pounding of her heart as she looked around her. No one acted as if Brant had done anything out of the ordinary. Even Kaylee wore a contented smile.

Focusing on the man who had just performed the most heroic act she'd ever seen, she watched him pick up a length of thick rope with a cowbell tied to it and hand it to Colt. The brothers exchanged a high five, and she could tell from their expressions that they'd put behind them their earlier disagreement about Colt riding the bull. Both men looked extremely pleased, and when the score for Colt's ride was flashed across the board, they grinned and slapped each other on the shoulder.

Amazed, Annie sat staring at the two brothers. They appeared to have enjoyed the excitement, the danger.

"Weren't you frightened for them?" she asked, turning to Kaylee.

The girl shook her head. "They both know what they're doing." Smiling, she pointed to a cowboy settling himself onto the back of a bull. "When riders get to this level of the PBR, they're the best in the world. Once they dismount, they all know they have to get to their feet as fast as they can and keep moving to get out of the way while the bullfighter distracts the bull. And Brant has always been the one bullfighter the guys want in the arena when they ride. They know they can depend on him to do everything in his power to divert the bull's attention so they can make it to safety."

Annie stared at Brant jogging over to once again take his position beside the bucking chutes. He'd proven his agility and athleticism by the way he'd adeptly avoided the bull his brother had ridden. And he certainly looked confident enough in what he was doing. She'd have to take it on faith that was the case.

During the course of the afternoon, Annie changed her mind several times about Brant. She couldn't decide whether he was the bravest man she'd ever met, or the most insane. Time after time, she watched him and the other two bullfighters save riders from the angry beasts by putting themselves in the paths of the dangerous animals. And they always managed to emerge from the skirmishes untouched.

But several hours later, after the last bull had trotted from the arena, and the crowd watched Kaylee's brother accept a hefty check for winning the event, Annie felt drained. She'd never witnessed anything as terrifying, exciting or oddly exhilarating as watching the cowboys and bullfighters pit their strength, courage and wits against two thousand pounds of angry animal.

"Well, it's time to find Mitch," Kaylee said, standing up to leave. She politely extended her hand. "It was really nice to meet you, Annie. Will I see you at next week's event?"

"I…I'm not sure," Annie said, joining Kaylee as they climbed the steps leading to the lobby area. "Will it be held here?"

Kaylee laughed. "No. The PBR won't be back here for another year. The guys are scheduled to be in Anaheim next weekend."

Annie didn't know what to say. Brant had said he was taking her with him, but she hadn't given a second thought as to where they would be going.

Suddenly feeling very unsure of her decision, she wondered what she'd gotten herself into. She was going off with a man she'd known less than twenty-four hours and didn't have a clue where he was taking her.

But before the gravity of what that might mean could sink in, a strong hand was placed to her back and a smooth baritone close to her ear asked, "So what did you think of your first bull riding event, sweetpea?"

A shiver coursed through her at the sound of Brant's voice and she glanced up to meet his incredibly blue gaze. A warm protected feeling surrounded her. She had no basis for trusting him, other than the integrity in his eyes and the fact that he'd been nothing but a gentleman from the moment they met.

He'd changed out of his outlandish garb, removed the greasepaint lines from around his mouth and eyes, and once again wore the wide-brimmed black Resistol that matched hers.

"Hey, there, Brant," Kaylee said from beside Annie. "You sure got your exercise today."

"Hi, Kaylee-Q." Brant reached out to affectionately pull the brim of the young woman's hat down over her eyes. "How's my favorite girl?"

"Happy. Mitch won today," Kaylee said, grinning as she repositioned her hat. "Now when I tell him I want that buckskin mare for my birthday that Joe Castleman has for sale, he can't use the excuse that he doesn't have any money."

Brant laughed. "You tell Mitch if he doesn't buy it for you, I won't be so quick to save his sorry hide the next time he lands flat on his back."

"I'll be sure to do that." Turning to Annie, Kaylee smiled. "I hope I see you in Anaheim."

"We'll see," Annie answered noncommittally.

As Kaylee disappeared into the crowd exiting the

lobby area, Brant steered Annie to a service elevator. "Where are we going?" she asked.

"We're taking the back way out of this place," he said, pushing the down button. "I don't want to take the chance that Elsworth is out front looking for you."

Annie shook her head. "He probably wouldn't think of looking for me here."

"Why?" Brant's grip tightened on the handle of his red-and-black duffel bag. Did she think this type of event was beneath her and old pasty-face?

"Because bull riding wouldn't appeal to him, therefore he wouldn't think it would be something I'd find entertaining." She pushed her glasses up with a brush of her hand as they stepped onto the elevator. The steel doors swished shut and the car began to descend. "Patrick never gave me credit for having any interests other than his."

"And is bull riding one of the things you find entertaining that he wouldn't?" Brant asked, not at all sure why her answer should matter to him.

He watched her nibble on her lower lip before answering. "I'm not sure." She glanced up at him. "I have to admit there were a couple of times this afternoon when I was scared witless."

"Why?"

"Because I was sure one of those bulls was going to run you down," she said, sounding genuinely concerned for his safety.

A warm feeling spread throughout Brant's chest, but he ignored the sensation. From what he'd seen, Annie was kind and didn't want to see anyone harmed in any way. She'd probably felt the same way about all the guys she'd seen in the arena today.

Before he could analyze why that thought disappointed him, the elevator doors opened and they stepped out into the same staging area they'd entered several hours before. Guiding Annie to the exit, Brant helped her into the back of a waiting cab, then gave the driver instructions to take them to Lambert airport.

"I know I should have inquired before, but where are we going?" she asked. He noticed that she nervously twisted the diamond ring she'd swiped from Elsworth the night before around her slender finger.

"We'll take a flight from here to Denver," he said, hoping to reassure her. "Then once we get my truck out of long-term parking, we'll spend the night and drive to the Lonetree tomorrow."

"Why aren't we flying directly to Cheyenne, or Casper, or wherever the closest airfield is to your ranch?" She twisted the ring a little more earnestly.

He placed his hand over hers. "I couldn't get a direct flight out of Cheyenne, so I drove down to Denver," he said, smiling. "It's only about a four hour drive."

"If it's that close, where are we staying tonight, and why?" She looked a little alarmed, and he could see the wheels turning in her pretty little head. Annie was speculating on what he had planned, and she wasn't sure she was going to like his answer.

"We'll get a couple of rooms close to the airport tonight, then after a shopping trip to get more clothes for you, we'll head home," he answered, hoping that his reference to two hotel rooms would put her more at ease.

"I hate for you to go to that expense," she said, gazing at him with guileless green eyes.

His heart slammed against his rib cage. Was she

saying she wanted him to get one room, that she wanted to spend the night with him?

Before he managed to find his voice, she went on, "Could you keep a total of what you spend so that my grandmother can reimburse you?"

Brant could have laughed at his own foolishness, if not for the disappointment settling in his gut. What the hell was wrong with him? Annie Devereaux wasn't his type of woman. She'd be about as comfortable doing the two-step in a honky-tonk as he'd be attending an opera where the people trying to sing sounded like cats with their tails caught in the door.

"I'm not worried about the cost, sweetpea," he said as the cab pulled up to the airport's east terminal.

He paid the driver, then helped Annie from the back seat and headed straight to the ticket counter. Discovering there wasn't another first-class seat available, he exchanged his ticket for business class, purchased one for Annie and checked his bag.

She waited until he pocketed his credit card before asking, "Do you always fly first-class?"

"When I can," he answered, placing his hand at her elbow. He steered her toward the area where the metal detectors were located. "The rows of seats are farther apart and I can straighten out my bad knee."

"You should have kept your seat," she said, stopping to glance back at the ticket counter. "Maybe you can get your ticket back if you—" She suddenly broke off whatever she'd been about to say and spun around to face forward.

Bewildered, Brant stopped walking and turned back to face her. She stood as if she'd been frozen to the spot, her face ghostly pale. "What's wrong?" he asked. When she remained silent, he placed his hands on her shoulders. "Annie?"

"I think I saw Patrick," she said, her voice little more than a whisper. "He's showing a picture to some people over by the ticket counter."

With a quick glance beyond the top of her head toward the check-in area, Brant swore. "That's him all right." The panic filling her pretty, green eyes twisted his gut. "Don't worry, sweetpea. I gave you my word that I wouldn't let him touch you, and I damn well intend to keep it." He held out his hand. "Let me have your glasses."

"What's he doing now?" she asked, handing them over.

"Don't turn around. It looks like he's working his way this direction," Brant said, tucking the black frames in his shirt pocket.

Taking her by the arm, he set his sights on the metal detectors up ahead. Fortunately, there weren't that many people waiting in line to go through the security check. Once they were past that point and into the gate area, Elsworth wouldn't be able to follow them without a ticket for one of the flights.

Before they even reached the detectors, Brant started digging his keys and change from his jeans pockets. He handed their tickets and boarding passes to the guard, then supported Annie by the elbow as she quickly tugged off her boots. While she sent them and her hat through the scanning device, he kicked off his shoes and removed his hat. Having to fly nearly every weekend to the various bull riding events, Brant was familiar with airport security and had quickly learned that when traveling, jogging shoes were easier to remove than having to pull off boots. He just wished that he'd thought of having Sarah pick up a pair of jogging shoes for Annie, instead of the boots.

Tossing his shoes and hat on the conveyer belt, he emptied the coins and keys from his hand into a small plastic container and followed Annie through the arched detector. He was relieved when neither one of them set off the alarm. That would have required a scan with a handheld device and given Elsworth more time to discover them.

While they waited for their things to clear the scanner, Brant looked over to where Elsworth stood talking to an airport custodian. He was still several yards away. Maybe they'd be out of sight before he got any closer.

No sooner had the thought crossed his mind, when Elsworth turned to stare in Brant and Annie's direction.

"Anastasia!"

At the sound of her name, Annie automatically turned around. "Oh my God," she whispered. "He's found us."

Brant stuffed his keys and change into his jeans, then leaning close, whispered into her ear, "Act like you don't know who he is. Just pick up your boots and hat and start walking." Jamming his own hat on his head, Brant grabbed his shoes, accepted the envelope with their tickets from the guard and ushered her down the causeway where their departure gate was located. "They won't allow him into this area without a boarding pass and ticket."

Annie glanced over her shoulder. Without her glasses she wasn't sure if Patrick's steely-eyed glare was real or a figment of her overactive imagination.

But it didn't matter. Whether the look was real or imagined, her heart pounded and it was all she could do to keep from breaking into a run. He was standing just on the other side of the security device and that was way too close for comfort.

When they reached their departure gate, and well out of Patrick's sight, Annie dropped her boots, sank into one of the seats and buried her face in her hands. "What have I gotten myself into?"

Brant sat down in the chair next to her to put on his shoes. "Everything is going to be fine, Annie. I gave you my word that Elsworth won't touch you." He turned to cup her cheek in his big palm, then staring at her with his startling blue eyes, he added, "And, sweetpea, if you knew me better, you'd know that's as ironclad as any contract a lawyer could draw up."

He held her gaze for several long seconds before dropping his hand and leaning down to tie his shoelaces. Rising to his feet, he turned toward the snack bar across from the waiting area. "I'm going to get a cup of coffee. Would you like something?"

Annie shook her head and watched as he strolled over to the kiosk, his gait loose and confident. There was no doubt in her mind that Brant meant every word he said. The only problem was, she wasn't sure she was any safer with him than she was with Patrick.

Oh, she knew for certain that Brant would never allow anyone or anything to harm her physically. It was her suddenly unstable emotions that concerned her. Every time he turned his incredible blue gaze her way, she felt things she'd never felt before. Her stomach fluttered as if a herd of butterflies had been unleashed, and heat streaked through her to areas that had no business warming up. If she didn't know herself better, she'd swear she had the hots for Brant Wakefield.

She shook her head to dislodge the unsettling thought. Anastasia Devereaux wasn't the type to have the hots for anyone. She was steady, dependable and never got excited about much of anything.

But what about Annie Devereaux? She'd walked an outside ledge high above the streets of Saint Louis, she'd spent the night in the same hotel suite with a man she didn't even know, and was about to spend the next week traveling, God only knew where, with him.

Annie swallowed hard. She was beginning to wonder if she still knew who she was. She'd always thought she was content with the life her grandmother had laid out for her. But now?

In the past twenty-four hours she'd had more excitement than she'd had in all of her twenty-four years. And, she'd never felt more alive.

Brant pushed the brim of his hat up with his thumb and glanced at the woman's head resting against his shoulder. They hadn't been in the air more than ten minutes, when Annie fell sound asleep. About five minutes after that, she'd moved to lean against him. He checked his watch. And they had another forty-five minutes left before the plane touched down in Denver.

He took a deep breath and the clean scent of her herbal shampoo surrounded him. It took everything he had in him to keep from reaching over to run his fingers through the pale-blond strands. She moved to a more comfortable position and he watched her perfect lips part on a soft sigh. His mouth suddenly felt as if it had been coated with cotton and he had to fight the urge to lean closer and press his lips to hers, to once again taste the sweetness of her.

That thought had him sitting up in his seat and staring straight ahead in two seconds flat. What the hell was wrong with him? Hadn't he learned the hard way that he had absolutely nothing in common with a woman like Annie?

He thought back to his college days when he'd been foolish enough to believe that an eastern, city-bred filly and a western, pasture-raised stud could work out the differences in their backgrounds and find lasting happiness. If not for the lingering pang of regret, he could almost laugh now about what an odd couple he and Daphne had been.

They'd met in an art appreciation class his senior year at the University of Wyoming. He'd needed another humanities course to graduate and she'd taken the class because that was the type of thing that appealed to her. He'd never been able to figure out why Daphne Elizabeth Morrison-Smythe had chosen to attend a state university out West, instead of one of the Ivy League schools closer to her home. Hell, they offered a lot more of that cultured stuff, and one of those schools even had a building named after her granddaddy.

But at the time, Brant hadn't cared. He'd taken one look at the flame-haired beauty and fallen head over heels in love. And he was pretty sure that she'd loved him too. At least, as much as she had been capable of loving.

Unfortunately, love hadn't been enough to bridge the gap in their backgrounds. She'd quickly tired of dressing in jeans and boots to watch him play chicken with a ton of pissed-off beef. Then she'd tried to convince him that he'd be just as happy dressed in a tux to attend a symphony or art exhibit as he was in his bullfighting gear. And for a while he'd tried. He really had.

But he'd had nothing in common with her highfalutin friends, and it hadn't taken him long to discover that trying to be something he's not just made him miserable. He couldn't change who he was any more than she could change who she was.

When they parted, it had been on amicable terms, but he'd learned a valuable lesson. People were going to have to accept him the way he was, or not. It was their choice. But he would never again try to change himself to please another person.

The ping of the seat-belt sign brought him back to the present. They were getting ready to land in Denver.

"Annie," he said softly, touching her shoulder.

"Mmm." She snuggled closer and smiled in her sleep. His chest tightened with a protective feeling like nothing he'd ever experienced.

"Sweetpea, the plane's getting ready to land."

Brant watched her long lashes flutter, then slowly open. He didn't think he'd ever seen anything quite so sexy.

When she tilted her head to look up at him, it must have registered with her that she'd used his shoulder for a pillow. Her cheeks coloring a pretty pink, she jerked upright. "How long have I been asleep?"

He chuckled. "I think you went out about the same time the seat belt sign did."

"I'm sorry," she said, finger-combing her hair.

Fascinated by the movement of the blond strands, it took a moment for Brant to realize what she'd said. "Sorry? For what?"

He noticed her finger shook slightly as she pointed to his sleeve. "I've wrinkled your shirt."

"Don't worry about it," he said, pulling her glasses from his shirt pocket. He wasn't going to upset her further by telling her that he'd actually enjoyed having her use him for a pillow. Hell, he wasn't all that comfortable with how much he'd liked it himself.

She put the black frames on, then pushed them up with a brush of her hand. "I've never been this far west as an adult."

Her simple statement reminded him that no matter how good it felt having her lean on him, or how protective he felt of her, they had nothing in common. "I'm sure it's going to be a lot different than you're used to," he said as the plane taxied to the terminal.

"Why do you say that?" she asked, covering her yawn with a delicate hand.

He swallowed hard. How would her hands feel on his body? Would they be as soft caressing and stroking his skin as he imagined?

Barely resisting the urge to cuss a blue streak, Brant gathered their coats and her hat from the overhead storage compartment, then waited until they'd disembarked the plane before he trusted himself to answer her. "There's a lot of distance between towns out here. And they're a lot smaller than where you're from."

"We have some pretty small towns in southern Illinois, too," she said as she walked ahead of him into the airport.

When a man bumped into her as he hurried toward

the baggage-claim area, Brant reached down and took her hand in his to keep them from being separated in the crowd. The bandage where he'd tended her scraped palm rubbed against his, reminding him of why she was with him. She was escaping a man that meant to harm her, not to approve or disapprove of the land he loved.

"Bear Creek is about twenty miles from the Lonetree. It's the closest town," he said as they waited for his duffel bag. "And about all there is in town is the grade school, a church, a bar and a general store with a lunch counter and a gas pump out front."

"What about a post office?" she asked, sounding genuinely interested. "Where's that located?"

"In the store." He plucked his red-and-black bag from the rest of the baggage. "The Rancher's Emporium carries everything from canned goods to tractor parts. And that includes a postal window."

"It sounds quite charming," she said, smiling up at him.

He laughed and shook his head as they stepped out of the terminal and waited for the shuttle to take them to long-term parking to get his truck. "I've heard Bear Creek called a one-horse town, a hole in the road, and a bump in a deer trail, but I think that's probably the first time anyone's ever called it charming."

Brant glanced out the lobby window at Annie, patiently waiting in the front seat of his truck for him to return with her room key. The only problem was, his room key and hers were one and the same.

He slid his wallet into his hip pocket and nodded to the middle-aged man behind the registration desk, then, taking a deep breath, walked back out to the pickup. Sliding into the driver's seat, he put the truck in gear and pulled around to the back of the building.

"We've got a slight problem," he said, cutting the engine and lights. "There was only one room available."

She calmly turned to face him. "How many beds?"

"Two."

"Good enough," she said, surprising him.

He got out and walked around to help her from the passenger's side. "You don't mind?"

"I'm too tired to care one way or the other," she admitted. "Besides, I know you can be trusted."

Inserting the key card in the lock, he held the door while she preceded him into the room, then turned back to the truck to get his bag. He wasn't exactly sure how Annie's statement made him feel. On one hand, he was honored that she trusted him so completely. On the other, he didn't care much for the idea that she thought of him as harmless either.

He slammed the truck door and headed back into the room. Hell, he was a flesh-and-blood man with a healthy appreciation for the opposite sex, just like any other. And the more time he spent around Annie, the more he appreciated the way her cute little rear swayed slightly when she walked, how her breasts filled out her new, tapered blouse.

"Do you want the shower first?" she asked when he closed the door and secured the locks.

"No, go ahead." He set his bag on the desk, then turned to find her looking at him expectantly. "What's wrong?"

"I need my skirt and blouse."

"Why?"

"It's the closest thing I have to a nightgown," she said as if it was the most reasonable explanation in the world.

Turning, he slid the heavy zipper open on the luggage, then handed her the clothes. "Here you go."

When she took them from him, something fell from between the two garments to land at his feet. Bending down, he picked up a scrap of beige lace with four straps dangling from it and a tiny patch of beige silk attached to an elastic waistband with something resembling a string.

Looking at the delicate items in his callused hands, Brant swallowed around the biggest wad of cotton he'd ever had clog his throat. Annie hadn't worn panty hose last night. She'd been wearing a garter belt and hose. And the mystery from this morning about what she did or didn't have on under her jeans had just been solved. Apparently, Annie had a thing for sexy underwear. *Very* sexy underwear.

Sweat popped out on his forehead and his body tightened in places that within seconds would be extremely hard and all but impossible to hide. "If you—" he stopped to clear the rust from his voice "—don't mind, I think I will take my shower first," he said, stuffing the delicate lingerie into her hands.

He didn't take time to rummage through his duffel for clean clothes. Instead, he picked the bag up by the handles and took it with him, then slamming the bathroom door behind him, dropped the luggage to the floor. Yanking the snaps free on his shirt, he quickly shucked the rest of his clothes, turned on the shower and without hesitation, stepped inside.

Barely suppressing his shocked yelp, Brant stood

beneath the icy spray until his teeth chattered and his
body felt as if it would never function properly again.

Her cheeks feeling as if they were on fire, Annie
stood with her fist clenched around the silk and lace
as she watched Brant close the bathroom door behind
him. This morning, when the woman he'd called
Sarah brought the items that he'd requested, Annie
had discreetly told her what she needed. Sarah had
understood completely and delivered the new underthings without blinking an eye. And although Brant
had looked extremely curious about their whispering,
he hadn't been the wiser.

But now, because of her carelessness, he had
learned the one thing about her that no one else besides Sarah knew. Annie preferred very delicate, very
provocative undergarments.

Sinking down on the end of the bed, she sighed.
She'd started wearing sexy lingerie in college as a
way of rebelling against her grandmother's strict up-
bringing. At the time, it had been the only thing she'd
had enough courage to do that was even close to wild
and daring. And the beauty of it was, it had been her
little secret. No one else knew that beneath her sensible khaki skirts and loose silk blouses she wore undergarments that were so sheer, so minuscule, she
might as well not be wearing anything at all.

She glanced toward the bathroom. At least until
now, no one else had known about it.

Staring at the closed door, she couldn't help but
grin. If the look on Brant's face was any indication,
the lingerie had been the very last thing he'd expected
to fall from her clothes. When he'd picked up her
thong and garter belt from the top of his shoe, his

sexy blue eyes had widened in utter shock and he'd been absolutely speechless.

Annie covered her mouth with her hand to keep from laughing out loud. Brant Wakefield had just learned that not everything was always as it seemed.

Even a stuffy, plain-Jane librarian had her little secrets.

Five

The next morning, Annie awoke to Brant's quiet snores coming from the other bed. Turning her head, she noticed that his black hair was slightly rumpled and his square jaw wore the dark shadow of overnight stubble. Instead of detracting from his good looks, it added a sexy ruggedness that sent a wave of goose bumps skipping over her skin. He really was one of the sexiest, best-looking men she'd ever met. And she was going to spend the next week going with him to heaven only knew where.

As she continued to watch him sleep, her gaze drifted lower and her eyes widened. When Brant had finally emerged from the bathroom last night, he'd been fully dressed and she could have sworn he was shivering when he climbed into bed and pulled the covers up to his ears. But sometime during the night, he'd pushed the covers down to his waist and removed his shirt.

Staring at the expanse of his chest as it rose and fell with his deep even breathing, she studied his perfect male body. His stomach and pectoral muscles were well defined, his skin smooth and inviting.

Her pulse quickened and she had to moisten her suddenly dry lips as the memory of what it felt like to be pressed to all that warm, hard sinew came rushing back. He'd held her so securely, so protectively when he'd rescued her from his balcony. What would it be like to be loved by a man like Brant, to have him caress her skin the way she'd touched his? Her lower belly fluttered and a tingling sensation coursed through her.

"That's it," she muttered, throwing the blanket back.

She rose from the bed and quietly crossed the short distance between the two beds. All that smooth, warm-looking male skin was enough to drive a saint to sin. It would definitely be in her best interest to cover him and stop all her foolish fantasizing about something that would never in a million years happen anyway.

But just as she reached down to pull the sheet up to cover his chest, Brant's hand grasped her wrist and tugged. Caught off balance, Annie tumbled forward and landed on top of him with a startled squeak.

"What's 'it'?" he asked, his sexy baritone rough with sleep. The sound sent a tremor coursing through her.

Annie couldn't think straight as she stared down into his vivid blue eyes. "Wh-what?"

He wrapped his arm around her shoulders and

turned them until she found herself lying flat on her back with him leaning over her. "You said, 'That's it' before you got up. What did you mean, sweetpea?"

She couldn't tell him that she'd been ogling his perfect body and savoring every luscious memory of what it felt like to touch him. Or that she'd been wondering what it would be like to have him touch her in ways she'd never been touched. "I...I don't remember."

"Liar," he said softly. He pillowed her head on his left forearm while he threaded the fingers of his right hand in her hair. "You were looking at my chest like a starving dog looks at a bone."

"You were watching?" she asked, wondering if that throaty female voice was really hers.

"Oh, yeah, sweetpea. There hasn't been a move you've made since you crawled into that bed last night that I haven't known about."

Her heart skipped a beat. "Really?"

He nodded. "Do you know how sweet you look when you sleep?"

"You were watching me?" she asked incredulously.

"Just like you were watching me." His smile caused the butterflies in her stomach to flap wildly.

Surely Brant didn't mean he was having the same kinds of thoughts about her that she'd been having about him. She just wasn't the type of woman that men wasted their time fantasizing about.

"I thought I'd cover you," she said, thinking fast. "You seemed to be a bit chilled last night after your shower."

His deep chuckle sent a shiver slithering up her

spine. "Sweetpea, do you know why I was so cold when I came out of the bathroom?"

"No," she said, moving her head back and forth.

Tracing his finger down her cheek to the fullness of her lower lip, he smiled. "I'd just spent a good ten minutes standing under a spray of ice-cold water."

Was he trying to tell her that she'd somehow aroused him? Not likely.

Her heart pounded against her ribs. "Why?"

He grinned. "I discovered that beige silk and lace can cause a man's temperature to rise considerably."

"It...does?" She'd known the sight of her underwear had surprised him, but she had no idea that it had affected him *that* way.

"You just about caused me to have a coronary last night, sweetpea," he said, nodding.

"Me?" Surely she misunderstood what he was saying.

The gleam in his stunning blue eyes as he nodded told her more than words that he meant everything he was telling her. "And you're doing a damn fine job of getting it jump-started this morning."

"Your heart?"

His deep chuckle sent heat streaking through her. "Among other things." He cupped her cheek with his hand as he gazed down at her. "Last night you told me you knew you could trust me."

"Y-yes." Annie couldn't believe how difficult it had suddenly become to form words.

"I just want you to know that although you can trust me, I'm not a gelding. I'm a man with a man's desires—susceptible to the same temptations as any other." His head slowly descended. "And right now, you're tempting me in ways that you can't even imagine, sweetpea."

"I find...that hard...to believe," she said, trying desperately to catch her breath.

"It's the truth." His firm mouth barely brushed hers. "But since it seems you have doubts, I guess I'll just have to show you." He raised his head to gaze down at her. "Do you want me to do that, Annie?"

She couldn't have stopped herself from nodding if her life depended on it. Heaven help her, but she wanted Brant to kiss her again. "Please."

His promising smile took her breath. "It'll be my pleasure, sweetpea."

As Brant's mouth covered hers, Annie's eyes drifted shut and she brought her hands up to run them over his wide, corded shoulders. His smooth warm flesh, the hardness of honed muscle beneath her palms, was everything she remembered and more.

His lips moved slowly, thoughtfully, over hers for endless seconds, as if giving her the opportunity to call a halt to the caress. But she could have no more stopped the kiss than she could pluck stars from the sky. She wanted Brant to kiss her, wanted to once again feel the exquisite pull of desire that she'd experienced in his arms the morning before.

His tongue traced the seam of her mouth and she answered his request by parting for him, allowing him entry. Strong and masterful, yet gentle and coaxing, his tender stroking created an eagerness in her that made her head spin. Gathering her courage, she tentatively touched her tongue to his and a groan rumbled up from deep in his chest. At the sound, a spark somewhere deep inside her flickered to life, then quickly grew into a flame. Heat spread to every part of her, and her limbs felt heavy and languorous.

Brant pulled her more fully against him, then slowly tugged her blouse from the waistband of her khaki skirt. Lifting the tail of the garment, he ran his callused palm over her skin, caressed her waist, her ribs, then the swell of her breast. When he moved to cup the heaviness, her heart skipped a beat and breathing seemed to be all but impossible.

He broke the kiss to nip and nibble his way to the rapidly beating pulse at the base of her throat. "Do you have any idea how sweet you are, Annie?" he murmured as his thumb chafed her nipple into a tight bud.

She shook her head. The many delicious sensations that Brant was creating inside her threatened to consume her and made any kind of speech impossible.

But when he pushed her blouse up to take the tight nub into his mouth, it felt as if an electric charge coursed through her. Her stomach tightened with an empty ache as he continued to tease the small bud, and a swirling heat began to pool at the juncture of her thighs.

So intense were the unfamiliar feelings, so breathtaking, she pushed against his shoulders. "Please… stop."

He raised his head and stared at her for several long moments, then cursing, rolled to the other side of the bed to sit up. "Annie, I—" He stopped to bury his head in his hands. "I never meant for things to go that far."

She suddenly felt as if she'd been dipped in ice water. Of course he hadn't meant it. A man like Brant was used to a woman with more finesse, more experience, not one who bolted at the first stirrings of desire. His back was to her, but she could just imagine the disgust in his expressive blue eyes.

Taking a deep breath, she tried to ignore the burning pain of disappointment as she rose from the bed. "Don't worry about it. I know I'm not the type that men fantasize about."

She gathered her jeans and shirt, then started to walk into the bathroom to change. But Brant's hand suddenly circled her upper arm and turned her to face him. How had he managed to get to his feet and round the bed so fast?

"Where the hell did you get that idea?" he asked, his frown formidable.

"I may wear glasses, but I'm not blind. When I look in the mirror, I can see that my hair looks like limp straw when it's down, and that my features are…ordinary." Shrugging one shoulder, she met his gaze head-on. "There's nothing about me that could be considered remarkable in any way."

Her eyes widened at the pithy phrase Brant blurted out. "Sweetpea, I don't know which mirror you've been looking into, but it's the wrong damn one."

"What do you mean?" she asked,

"Your hair looks and feels like spun silk," he said, reaching out to stroke the blond strands. Smiling, he cupped her chin with his hand, then gently chafed her lower lip with the pad of his thumb. "Your eyes are a beautiful shade of emerald, your lips are perfectly shaped." He grinned. "And they felt pretty damn remarkable both times I've kissed you."

Her heart skipped a beat as she gazed up at him. "They did?"

Nodding, he stared at her for what seemed an eternity, then quickly stepped back. "Now, get changed so we can get out of here. Otherwise, I might forget that I'm supposed to be playing the part of a trustworthy gelding, instead of a man who would like nothing more than to get you back in that bed and kiss you again." His smile curled her toes and caused a heaviness to pull at her lower stomach. "And more."

As they left the outskirts of Denver, Brant set the cruise control, then glanced over at Annie. She was busy sorting through all the shopping bags from their trip to the mall and the western-wear store.

When she held up a bag from the Sleek and Sassy Lady Lingerie Boutique, and started rummaging through it, he swallowed hard, fixed his eyes on the road ahead and kept them there. That was the one store he hadn't gone into with Annie. He hadn't dared. Just the thought of her choice of underthings still made him break out in a sweat and had him imagining all sorts of scenarios. And every one of them ended with him removing scraps of silk and lace.

Brant gripped the wheel and clenched his teeth. He'd made a damn fool of himself last night when her garter belt and panties—if they could be called panties—fell at his feet. Then he'd made an even bigger fool of himself this morning when he'd let his hormones override his good sense. But Annie's lips were the sweetest, sexiest he'd ever had the pleasure of kissing. And, he decided, could quickly become an addiction if he wasn't careful.

He concentrated on breathing in and out for several seconds. Ten years ago he'd made a vow to steer clear of women like Annie. He had nothing in common with them. Something deep in his gut kept telling him that Annie was different, that she wasn't the same type of woman as Daphne. And what disturbed him the most was, he found himself hoping his instincts were on target—that she was nothing like Daphne.

"How are the new contacts?" he asked in an effort to take his mind off the direction his thoughts had strayed. After Annie had finished shopping, she'd asked him to take her to one of the vision-care chain stores. "Are you getting used to them?"

"Actually, I think I like them very much," she said, sounding happy. "Thank you for mentioning them."

A warm feeling spread throughout his chest. It felt good to make her happy. Too good.

Clearing his throat, Brant searched for something else to say. "Did you get everything you'll be needing for the next week?"

Placing the sacks at her feet, she sighed. "I forgot to buy something to sleep in."

"I'll stop in Cheyenne," he said, trying not to think about what her choice of sleepwear looked like.

She remained silent for a moment. "You've spent so much on me already, I really hate for you to spend more."

He chuckled. "It's not a problem, sweetpea."

"That's what you keep saying." She paused. "Do you have some old T-shirts? I could sleep in one of them."

Brant decided it had to have been a miracle that kept him from steering the truck off into the ditch at Annie's suggestion. His heart pounded and his stomach muscles tightened at the thought of her sleeping in one of his shirts. For some strange reason, he liked the idea more than just a little bit.

"Uh, fine by me. But are you sure you don't want me to stop in Cheyenne?"

She nodded. "I'm sure. That way you won't have to spend more money."

He was getting tired of her worrying about him spending money. "Annie, this is the last time we're going to talk about this. I can more than afford to buy as many clothes as you want."

"Well, I still intend to pay you back after I return home," she said stubbornly.

"No, you won't."

"Yes, I will."

"Like hell." He pulled the truck onto the shoulder of the interstate, killed the engine, then turned to glare at her. "Let's get this settled once and for all. You're not going to pay me back. I bought the clothes for you, you're going to wear them and that's it."

"But—"

"No buts about it, lady."

She stared back at him for a moment before finally giving in with a sigh. "Okay, whatever you say."

"I'm glad we have that settled," he said, leaning over to plant a quick kiss on her perfect lips. "Now, let's get home. I'd like you to see the Lonetree before it gets dark."

As he pulled back onto the interstate, it bothered him that Annie thought he couldn't afford what they'd bought. Didn't she think he was successful at what he did? Did she think that just because he preferred jeans and boots, his standard of living was below hers?

Hell, he didn't flaunt the fact that his bank account

was well into the six-figure column. Truth be told, he didn't even care. He worked hard, led a fairly simple life, and wouldn't have it any other way.

Concentrating on the road ahead, Brant tried to ignore the disappointment settling in his chest and the tight knot forming in his stomach. Had his gut instinct been wrong? Was Annie really as materialistic as Daphne had turned out to be?

Annie had no idea why Brant was so adamant about her not reimbursing him, or why he'd gotten so upset. She only wanted to make sure he knew she wasn't trying to take advantage of his generosity.

Deciding his attitude must have something to do with male pride, she gazed out the truck window at the snow-covered scenery and mentally calculated how much they'd spent in the various stores. He might think he'd convinced her to drop the idea of paying him back, but he was in for a big surprise. She'd been raised by Carlotta Whittmeyer, the most stubborn, headstrong woman in southern Illinois. And this was one of the few areas where she and her granddaughter were just alike. Brant Wakefield might think he'd won this one, but he hadn't. He would get his money back, whether he liked it or not.

Her decision made, Annie settled back to enjoy the view. The mountains were, in a word, breathtaking. "It's beautiful out here, Brant."

"You've never seen the Rockies?" he asked, sounding shocked.

She shook her head. "Not really. My mother and father brought me out here on a camping trip when I was very small, but I don't remember anything about it." An ache settled in her chest at the thought of her parents and how much they'd missed together as a family. "After they died, my grandmother wouldn't allow me to travel very often, and never anywhere that she thought would pose a danger."

Brant reached over and clasped her hand. "I'm sorry, sweetpea. I remember you said they'd been killed." He tenderly traced his thumb over the back of her hand. "I lost my mom right after she had Colt, then Dad died ten years later."

"How old were you?" she asked, gently squeezing his hand. His callused palm against hers felt reassuring, and a warm secure feeling spread throughout her being.

"I was six when Mom died and almost seventeen when Dad got killed in a ranching accident." He drew her hand up to his mouth, then kissed the back of it. "But at least I had Morgan and Colt."

She'd always wanted a brother or sister. What she'd gotten was her grandmother's cranky cat, Sherlock. "The three of you are close, aren't you?"

He nodded. "Oh, we have our arguments like all brothers do, but there's nothing we wouldn't do for each other. We know that whenever one of us needs something, all we have to do is let the other two know."

"That must be nice," she said, unable to keep the wistfulness from her voice.

They fell into a companionable silence for some time before Brant turned the truck off the highway and onto another road. "We just crossed the Lonetree's eastern boundary," he said, smiling fondly.

Annie looked around. She didn't see a house. "How far is your home from the main road?"

"About six miles as the crow flies," he said, chuckling at her obviously shocked expression.

"Brant, how big is this ranch?"

"A little over a hundred and fifty thousand acres," he said, stopping the truck at the top of a rise.

Her eyes widened. "That's a lot of land."

Shrugging, he pointed to the valley below them. "There's ranch headquarters."

Annie's eyes widened. One of the biggest, most beautiful log homes she'd ever seen sat at one end of the valley, close to several barns and sheds. Smoke rose from a large stone chimney as if beckoning those who lived there to come into its warmth. The fields surrounding the place were blanketed with snow, and the approaching shadows of twilight as the sun slid behind the mountains in the distance created a scene that could have easily been featured on a Christmas card.

"My God, Brant, it's gorgeous," she said, sitting forward.

"You really like it?" he asked, sounding skeptical.

She turned to face him. "I love it. How long has your family owned the Lonetree?"

Smiling, he shifted the truck into drive and slowly drove down the snowpacked lane. "The Wakefields settled here a hundred and fifteen years ago this summer."

"Is the house that old?" It looked a lot larger and more modern than what someone would have built in the nineteenth century.

He laughed. "Somewhere in there I'm sure the old cabin still exists. But each generation has added more to it."

He turned onto a driveway with a square arch over

it. The sign hanging from the wooden structure had Lonetree Ranch painted in the center and symbols on either side that Annie assumed to be ranch brands.

"See the section on this side of the porch?" he asked. "Morgan had that added two years ago."

"There wasn't already enough room for the three of you?" Annie asked incredulously.

"Morgan wanted a room for the pool table and big-screen TV," Brant answered, parking the truck at the side of the house. "There's even enough room for three recliners and a big couch, too."

"Oh, the loungers are certainly a must," she said, laughing.

He reached down to release the latch on his shoulder belt, then did the same with hers. Tugging her over to the center of the bench seat, he wrapped his arms around her. "Hey, lady, when you have a busted leg, those things are darned nice."

Her smile faded. "You've had a broken leg?"

"I've broken one leg and torn up the ACL on the other knee," he said as he threaded his fingers in her hair.

"ACL?"

"Anterior cruciate ligament," he explained with a smile.

"Was that from fighting bulls?" she asked breathlessly.

"The torn ACL was. The broken leg was from falling off a hay wagon when I was thirteen."

"Who took care of you?" she said, touching his lean cheek with her hand.

"My brothers when they weren't busy with chores," he answered, his hand cupping the back of her head. "Most of the time, I took care of myself."

"You should have had someone with you all the time," she said, her heart aching at the thought of him being hurt and left alone to fend for himself while his brothers tended the ranch. She told herself she'd feel that way about anyone who'd been injured. But she suspected the feeling was more intense because she knew that Brant had been the one in pain.

His intense blue gaze caught hers and held it as he stared down at her. "Would you take care of me if I got hurt, sweetpea?"

Without a moment's hesitation she nodded. But before she had a chance to think about her hasty agreement, Brant groaned and pulled her head forward. Settling his mouth on hers, he hungrily tasted her lips, tugging gently on her lower lip with his teeth.

A tingling sensation started in her limbs and quickly spread to every part of her body. Drugging in its intensity, the feeling quickly settled in the pit of her stomach to form a rapidly tightening coil.

As wave after wave of excitement coursed through her, Annie lifted her arms to wrap them around his neck. Tangling her fingers in the thick black hair brushing his collar, she held him close and took pleasure in once again being kissed by the sexiest man she'd ever known. But when Brant slipped his tongue between her lips to stroke the inner recesses of her mouth, the coil in her belly tightened to a heated ache and an emptiness deep inside caused her to shift restlessly.

Wanting more of his touch, she reached up to take his hand from the back of her head and placed it on her breast. Had she been able to think straight, she would have been appalled at her wanton actions. But rational thought was beyond her capabilities. All she wanted was to feel his hands on her again.

"Ah, sweetpea." He gently kneaded the sensitive mound through the fabric of her cotton shirt. "You feel so damn good."

The sound of a truck pulling to a halt beside them, then seconds later the rap of knuckles on the driver's window, sent a chill up Annie's spine. Before she could jerk away from Brant, he tightened his arm around her as he slowly moved his hand down to her waist.

"Excuse me, sweetpea, but I have a brother to strangle." Turning, he opened the window. "What the hell do you want, Morgan?"

"Sorry to break up the fun, but I need your help," a deep voice said. From her vantage point, Annie couldn't see Brant's brother, but he sounded as if he might be in pain.

She heard Brant groan as he moved to get out of the truck. "How did you jerk your shoulder out of joint this time?" he asked. "You know I hate when I'm the one who has to pop it back in place."

Annie looked around Brant at the man standing next to the truck, holding his limp left arm close to his side. Morgan Wakefield was every bit as good-looking as both of his brothers and had the same intense blue eyes. But strain lines bracketed his mouth and she could tell that he was hurting.

"I went over to check on the Shackley place and fell through a rotten board on the porch step," Morgan said, backing up for Brant to get out of the truck. "I hit my shoulder on one of the support posts." He muttered a curse. "And believe me, you don't hate having to do this nearly as much as I hate having to have it done.''

"Shouldn't he see a doctor?'' Annie asked, scrambling out of the truck behind Brant.

Both men shook their heads. "Big brother, here, dislocated his shoulder a few years back, but instead of having surgery to fix the problem, he just lets it slip out of joint on a regular basis.'' Brant snorted. ''And Colt and I get the pleasure of popping it back in for him.''

"Quit your moaning and let's get this over with,'' Morgan said through gritted teeth. ''It's not out of joint completely this time.''

"House or barn?'' Brant asked.

"Barn,'' Morgan said, turning to walk toward one of the well-kept structures several yards away.

Brant placed his hands on her shoulders. ''It might be best if you stay here, sweetpea. This isn't something you're likely to want to see or hear.'' He grimaced. ''Hell, it's not something I want to witness.'' Pressing a quick kiss to her lips, Brant turned and followed Morgan.

Annie watched the two brothers disappear into the barn. All three of the Wakefield men were tall, had the same impossibly wide shoulders and narrow hips, and were extraordinarily handsome. But there was something about Brant that was different. Maybe it was his easygoing manner, his engaging smile.

As she stood pondering what she found so enchanting in Brant that his brothers might lack, a loud shout, followed by rapid, unintelligible phrases came from the barn. Seconds later, Brant sauntered out of the big double doors and walked over to where she stood by his black truck.

"Is your brother all right?" she asked, alarmed that Brant would leave Morgan in such obvious pain.

"Yeah, he'll be okay." Brant opened the truck and handed her the shopping bags, while he grabbed his duffel bag. "It's best we go inside and let Morgan get the cussing out of his system." Chuckling, Brant shook his head. "If we don't, your tender sensibilities are going to end up being offended—real quick."

When Annie heard a very clear, extremely graphic word come from the barn, she grinned. "I think you might be right about going into the house."

He frowned and hurried her up the porch steps. "That was just the warm-up. In another second or two he's going to cut loose with the really creative stuff." Brant seemed to take a deep breath as he reached for the doorknob. "It's probably not as fancy as what you're used to, but welcome to the Lonetree Ranch, sweetpea."

Six

Brant held the door for Annie to precede him into the house. He wondered if she'd like the rustic, western decor of the Lonetree ranch house, or if she'd be like Daphne and start making suggestions about how much better it would look with this piece of furniture or that work of art.

"Brant, your home is beautiful," Annie said, wandering from the foyer into the great room. He heard her suck in a sharp breath at the fire blazing in the big stone fireplace. "I love this. It's perfect for the room."

When she turned to face him, he caught the first glimpse of her expression and he could tell that she meant every word she'd said. "You don't find it a little too rustic?" he asked cautiously.

"Not at all." Her eyes bright with enthusiasm, she reached out to run her fingers over the colorful Native

American throw on the brown leather couch. "It couldn't be more appropriate."

Why her opinion of his home should matter, Brant didn't have a clue. But Annie's appreciation for the Lonetree ranch house caused warmth to fill his chest and the tension that he hadn't even realized gripped his shoulders to ease.

Shrugging out of his jacket, he helped her out of hers, then plucked the hat from her head. "Make yourself at home while I go hang these on the pegs by the door."

When he walked back into the room, Annie had dropped the shopping bags on the floor and was seated on the couch, running her hand along the blue slate top of the coffee table. "This is a very unusual piece of furniture," she said, smiling up at him. "I really like it. Who thought of placing a slab of stone on top of a tree stump?"

"I think my mom and dad came up with that idea in self-defense." He laughed when she arched a perfectly shaped eyebrow. "When Morgan and I were young, we had these trucks that we used to love running along the top of Mom's coffee table. They really tore up the finish, not to mention got us in a heap of trouble. By the time Mom got pregnant with Colt, she'd made Dad refinish the table twice. I guess they figured with three kids in the house they'd go broke buying new stain and varnish, so they put their heads together and this is what they came up with."

"That's a wonderful story," Annie said, sounding wistful. "I wish I had memories like that."

"Your grandmother didn't allow you to play like a normal kid?"

Shaking her head, she smiled sadly. "I had a playroom upstairs and wasn't allowed to have my toys in any other part of the house.''

''Why?''

''I think Grandmother had the idea that I would scratch her antiques or clutter up the rest of the house with them.''

Brant stared at her for several seconds before pulling her up from the couch and into his arms. He'd never known what it was like not to be allowed to be a kid, not to feel as if the house he lived in was home. He'd always had a close family, and after their parents died, he and his brothers had grown even closer.

But Annie had never had that. She'd gone to live with her grandmother after her parents' deaths. From what he could gather about the old woman, she'd never made Annie feel as if she had a home.

''I'm sorry, sweetpea,'' he said, stroking her silky hair. ''It must have been lonely, playing in that room all by yourself.''

She surprised him when she shook her head. ''It really wasn't all that bad, actually.'' Her smile lit his soul. ''I was much happier in my playroom than I was in the mausoleum Grandmother wanted to call a house.''

He chuckled. ''That bad, huh?''

''Oh, yes.'' Her smile faded and she shuddered against him. ''All the furniture was dark and dreary.'' She turned her head to look around the great room, before she turned back to gaze up at him. ''It's nothing like this. Your home feels warm and friendly. Like a family lives here. My grandmother's home has always been more like a Victorian museum.''

Brant didn't know what to say. But the thought of Annie as a lonely little girl, discouraged from feeling that her grandmother's house was her home, made his stomach churn. A protective feeling swept through him that damn near took his breath, not to mention scared the hell out of him.

Annie wasn't his type. She was books and art, charity fund-raisers and plays. He was rodeo and ranching, smoky honky-tonks and country music.

But their differences didn't seem to matter to his libido when she wrapped her arms around his waist and rested her head against his chest. Holding her close was playing hell with his vow to keep his distance, but he could no more step away from her than a buffalo could roost in a tree. Something about Annie made him want to make it up to her for her lousy childhood, had him wanting to keep her from ever being lonely again.

"Brant, don't you think the lady might like to see her room and freshen up before supper?" Morgan asked, breaking into Brant's disturbing thoughts. "Although, come to think of it, she doesn't look nearly as hungry as you do."

Glancing up, Brant saw his brother standing in the doorway leading into the kitchen, his left arm in the sling they kept for the times when his shoulder popped out of joint. Morgan wore a smug smile that set Brant's teeth on edge. If he could have reached his brother, he would have throttled him right then and there.

"Annie, I don't think I introduced you to my older brother, Morgan," Brant said, releasing her. He reached down to gather the shopping bags she'd set on the floor, along with his duffel bag. "He's also known as the smart-mouth Wakefield." Heading for the stairs, Brant added, "Morgan, this is my friend,

Annie Devereaux. She'll be staying here until we take off for Anaheim.''

"Nice to meet you, Annie," Morgan said, nodding his head.

"It's nice to meet you too," Annie said, smiling.

Brant stood back and let her precede him up the log-planked stairs to the second floor, then followed her. The irritating sound of Morgan's deep chuckle had Brant casting a murderous glare over his shoulder. "I'll see you in the office after supper."

Morgan laughed out loud. "I'll be looking forward to it, little brother."

Two hours later, Brant found Morgan sitting behind the desk in the study, his boots propped on the edge of the polished walnut surface. He used the long-neck bottle of beer he held to motion for Brant to pick up one just like it on the other side of the desk.

"So what's the word on the Shackley heir?" Brant asked, taking the bottle and sinking into one of the leather armchairs. "Have the lawyers found her yet?"

Morgan frowned. "Yes, and no."

Brant took a long draw on his bottle. "You want to explain that one?"

"Yes, they found Tug's daughter." Morgan shook his head. "In a cemetery."

"Then what happens to Tug's ranch?" Brant asked, sitting forward. "Does that mean we'll be able to buy it? Or will the law firm put it up for auction?"

"Neither."

Brant blew out a frustrated breath. There were times when getting details out of Morgan was like trying to sweet-talk a donkey into going somewhere he didn't want to go. "I assume there's a reason the ranch won't go up for sale?"

Morgan nodded. "The woman had a daughter."

"So she doesn't want to sell?"

"They don't know because they can't find her." Morgan leaned his head back against the high back of the leather desk chair. "All they know for sure is that she's somewhere between Seattle and San Diego."

Whistling low, Brant shook his head. "That covers a lot of territory."

"Yeah, and in the meantime, I'm stuck with keeping an eye on the place." Morgan took a swig of his beer. "Enough about my trying to buy out our dead neighbor's property. How did Colt do in Saint Louis?"

Brant shrugged. "He made his first two rides, but he lost the rope about three seconds into his final ride and I had to save his butt again. He ended up in third place, overall."

"So he managed to keep from getting hurt this time?" Morgan asked.

"Not exactly." Brant set his empty beer bottle on the desk. "He did a header dismount off his first bull and suffered another concussion."

Grinning, Morgan shook his head. "Well, it's a good thing he landed on his head. Otherwise he might have really hurt himself."

"Yeah, but his brains are going to be mush," Brant said, laughing.

"I didn't know he had any to begin with," Morgan said dryly. When they stopped laughing, Morgan asked, "By the way, where is our baby brother?"

"He went home with Mitch Simpson. He's going

with Mitch to buy Kaylee's birthday present.'' At Morgan's lifted eyebrow, Brant held up his hands. ''Don't ask me. He keeps saying she's nothing but a kid.''

Morgan shook his head. ''Kids grow up.''

Nodding, Brant rested the ankle of one leg on the knee of the other. ''She already has.'' He shook his head. ''Kaylee's grown into a really nice-looking young woman.''

Morgan eyed him for several long seconds, then asked what Brant had been waiting for. ''Speaking of nice-looking ladies, what's the story with the cute little blonde upstairs?''

The fact that Morgan found Annie attractive had Brant feeling both pleased and irritated at the same time. And he wasn't sure why.

''She needed a place to stay for a week.''

''Is that it?'' Morgan asked, looking skeptical.

''She's in a little trouble,'' Brant admitted. Filling his brother in on how he'd met Annie and why she was on the run, he finished with, ''You wouldn't have left her to deal with that pasty-faced little bean counter, either.''

Morgan shook his head. ''Nope.'' He looked thoughtful for a moment. ''But from what I saw earlier, there's more to the story than you're telling.''

''No way,'' Brant protested. ''She's from the same type of background as Daphne. And we both know what a disaster that turned out to be. I'm just trying to help her out of a bind, that's all.''

''Anything you say, brother.''

''Really.''

''Sure.''

Morgan's knowing grin had Brant wishing he had

another chance to jerk on his brother's sore shoulder. Rising to his feet, he headed for the door. He called Morgan a name as he walked out into the hall that had his brother laughing so hard he'd probably fall out of his chair. At that moment, nothing would have made Brant happier.

He might be attracted to Annie, but that's as far as Brant intended for it to go. She was from a different world than his, and he'd been shown in the past that those worlds tended to collide.

Brant decided not to dwell on it as he climbed the stairs, entered his room and headed for the shower in his private bathroom. In a week, he'd turn Annie over to her grandmother's care and get on with his life.

But long after he stretched out on the bed, he lay staring at the ceiling, thinking about the kisses he'd shared with Annie and the fact that she was lying just down the hall in one of his T-shirts. She kissed with a shy passion that was quickly becoming an addiction for him. What would it be like to hold Annie's sweet body to his? To take his shirt off her and feel himself sinking into her softness, to bring her to the brink, then take her into a realm where their backgrounds didn't matter? Would she make love with the same innocent enthusiasm as she did when she kissed him?

His lower body hardened to an almost painful state as his hormones kicked into overdrive, along with his overactive imagination. Curses hot enough to peel paint rolled off his tongue as he kicked off the blankets and headed back into the bathroom. Turning on the cold-water tap, he stepped beneath the icy spray.

His teeth chattering like a set of out-of-control castanets, Brant decided that one of two things would happen by the time he took Annie to her home in

Illinois. He'd come down with a really nasty cold, or he'd end up being a raving maniac with a perpetual arousal.

He glanced down at his stubborn body. Or with his luck, he'd end up in a constant state of arousal, as well as coughing his head off from double pneumonia.

Annie yawned for the third time as she stood looking out the window in the great room at the mountains in the distance. She'd spent a sleepless night wondering if she might not be running from the wrong man. Brant represented everything in life she'd been taught to avoid. He thrived on taking risks and tempting fate every time he stepped into a rodeo or bull riding arena.

But whether she'd been cautioned to avoid his type or not, she'd felt more exhilarated, more alive in the past three days than she'd ever felt in her life. And whether it was wise or not, she found herself more than just a little attracted to him. That's why she'd tossed and turned throughout the night. She'd analyzed it over and over and came to the same conclusion each time. She was falling for him.

Sighing heavily, she traced her finger along the window facing. Each time he kissed her, she found herself not only wanting his lips on hers, she wanted to feel his warm masculine skin pressed against her, wanted to explore his body and have him explore hers.

She shifted from one foot to the other. There was no sense in denying it. She wanted Brant.

What would it be like having him hold her against

his big, hard body? How would it feel to have him make love to her?

"What are you thinking about, sweetpea?" he asked, walking up behind her.

It was all Annie could do to keep a nervous giggle from erupting as she turned to face him. If he only knew the direction her thoughts had taken, he'd be shocked right down to the soles of his cowboy boots.

"Nothing really," she said, smiling. "I was just enjoying the beautiful view."

Glancing over the top of her head, he nodded. "I've always liked looking at the Shirley Mountains from that window." He looked back down at her and his charming grin curled her toes inside her new boots. "How would you like to go play in the snow?"

"I've never done that," she said, returning his smile. "It sounds like it might be fun."

"Never?"

She shook her head. "No. We don't get that many deep snows in southern Illinois, and if we did get snowfall deep enough, my grandmother was always afraid I'd get sick if I went out to play."

He put his arms around her waist and drew her close. "Well, you're not a little girl anymore, Annie," he said gently. "You can do whatever you want now."

Annie had to blink back the tears that threatened to spill down her cheeks as she stared up at him. Brant was the first person since her parents' deaths to encourage her to do what made her happy, to be herself.

"Thank you," she said, rising on tiptoe to place a kiss on his firm lips.

He looked confused. "For what?"

"For letting me be me."

"I like watching you be you," he said, lowering his head to cover her mouth with his.

As soon as his firm lips touched hers, Annie felt the familiar tingling begin to thread its way through every part of her body as it made its way to the pit of her stomach. Heat quickly followed and caused an empty ache to pool at the apex of her thighs. When his tongue coaxed her to open for him, her eagerness for him to deepen the kiss stole her breath. She wanted to feel him taste her again, wanted him to stroke the tender recesses of her mouth.

Brant moved his hands from her waist to pull her hips into the cradle of his, and the evidence of his strong arousal pressed to her lower belly caused her knees to feel as if they would no longer support her. Putting her arms around his neck, she clung to him with an abandon that shocked her. She'd never before been the passionate type. But in the circle of Brant's arms she seemed to transform from a shy, unassuming woman into a wanton who knew exactly what she needed.

The thought brought her up short and had her pushing against his shoulders to break the kiss. "I…I don't know what came over me," she said, wondering if that husky tone really belonged to her.

"Sweetpea, don't ever apologize for kissing like that," Brant said, his breathing harsh. Seeming to understand that she needed time to come to terms with this new sexual side of herself, he loosened his hold and put a bit of space between them. He cleared his throat. "So what do you say? Wanna go play in the snow?"

She took a deep breath, then gazed up into his vivid blue eyes. "Yes," she said, managing a smile. "Are we going to build a snowman or have a snowball fight?''

He laughed. ''We can do those things after we get back.''

''Where are we going?''

''You'll see,'' he said, pressing his lips to her forehead. Stepping back, he took her hand in his and led her to the stairs, then patted her bottom to urge her up the steps. ''Go get the mittens and sunglasses you bought in Denver yesterday, while I get our coats and hats.''

Brant watched Annie until she disappeared in the loft above, then turned to find Morgan standing right behind him. ''What are you grinning at?'' he asked, irritated at his brother's smug expression.

''You and that little lady are just friends, huh?'' Morgan asked, rocking back on his heels.

''Yes.''

Morgan threw back his head and laughed like a hyena. ''Keep telling yourself that if you want to, but I think we both know better.''

Brant was used to his brother's teasing. But this time, Morgan's sly observations were hitting a little too close for comfort. He was starting to feel things for Annie that were way across the line of a mere friendship.

''You think you're pretty damn smart, don't you?'' Brant asked, his back teeth clenched so tightly he felt as if they were welded together.

''Smart enough to see what the score is on this one,'' Morgan said, strolling into the foyer. He chuckled. ''You'd better start deciding which one of us you want to be the best man, me or Colt.''

"I think you hit your head, along with your shoulder yesterday," Brant growled, following his brother.

"Just let me know in time to get a haircut," Morgan said, giving Brant an irritating grin as he disappeared through the office door.

"Don't hold your breath," Brant muttered, lifting the lid on a chest beneath the pegs where he'd hung his and Annie's coats and hats the evening before.

"Were you talking to me?" Annie asked, descending the stairs.

Brant removed two Native American blankets and placed them on top of the chest, then turned to watch her cross the great room. "Nah, Morgan was being a smart-mouth again."

She smiled. "It must be nice to have a sibling to joke with."

He snorted. "Yeah, there are times when it's so much fun, I can hardly stand it," he said, holding her coat while she slipped her arms into the sleeves. Shrugging into his own jacket, he put on his hat, then took a sock cap from one of the other pegs and pulled it on top of her head. "We'll be gone for a couple of hours and I want you staying warm." He smiled at her. "Did you remember the sunglasses?"

"Right here," she said, holding up a pair of wire-rimmed frames with dark lenses. "I assume these are to keep from being blinded by the glare from the snow?"

"Yep." He put on his own pair of shades, grabbed the blankets, then took her hand in his. "As soon as we get Dancer, we'll be ready to go."

"Dancer?"

"My horse."

Annie stopped dead in her tracks. "We're riding a horse?"

"Is that a problem?"

"I've never ridden one," she said, nibbling on her lower lip.

Brant grinned. "You've never played in the snow either, but that's not stopping you, is it?"

He loved watching the sparkle of excitement fill her pretty, green eyes. "No, it's not," she said decisively. She put her sunglasses on, then flashed him a smile that sent his blood pressure up a few dozen points. "This is going to be a day filled with firsts for me. And I can't wait."

Ten minutes later, Brant placed one of the blankets on Dancer, then turned to Annie. "Ready?"

"I—" She stopped to give the gelding an apprehensive look. "Yes, but how do I get up there?"

"Just like this," he said, placing his hands around her small waist. Lifting her, he sat her astride the horse's broad back.

"Oh my God, I can't believe I'm doing this," she said, clutching the other blanket so hard he figured she'd squeeze the bright colors right out of it.

"Just relax," he said, grabbing the reins and a handful of mane to launch himself up behind her. "Now spread the blanket over your legs so you stay warm."

She did as he said, then asked, "Is there anything else I'm supposed to do?"

"Just enjoy the ride," he said, wrapping an arm around her waist to pull her to him.

But when her delightful little bottom came into contact with his groin as she settled herself against him, it was all Brant could do to keep from groaning out loud. Swallowing hard, he nudged Dancer into a slow walk out of the barn and across the ranch yard.

"I'm actually riding a horse," Annie said, laughing delightedly.

"You sure are, sweetpea." He pressed a kiss to the side of her head. "Are you comfortable?"

She wiggled her bottom back against him a little more, then nodded. "Now I am."

Brant felt as if his heart might pound a hole right through his rib cage. Annie's small body touching his from knees to shoulders was sending his hormones racing through him at an alarming rate and gathering in the region just below his belt. His palms turned sweaty inside his leather gloves. Damn! They hadn't even made it to the lane yet and he was already hard as hell.

He'd purposely decided to ride Dancer bareback because heat from the horse's body would help keep them warm. But he hadn't given a thought to what the friction from Annie's body would do to his. As the gelding plodded along the snowplowed lane, Annie's backside rubbed against his groin and had him clenching his teeth with vise-grip force.

They remained silent as they rode down the lane, then started down another road. The air was crisp and cold, but the sun shone brightly, sparkling like diamonds on the surface of the snow covering the landscape.

"Brant, this is absolutely breathtaking," Annie said, turning to look over her shoulder at him.

"You should see it in the spring when everything is new and green," he said, managing a smile. "Wildflowers cover the fields and everywhere you look you can see a mama with a new baby."

"I'd love to see this countryside in spring," Annie said, sounding sincere.

A warmth filled his chest at the thought of having Annie with him to watch the seasons change. But he ignored it. He knew better than to count on her staying around to see the flowers bloom, or the lanky little pronghorn and mule deer jumping and frisking around the valleys while their mamas grazed on the new growth. In a week she'd be going back to Illinois and her cultured way of life. And he'd stay right where he was, because that's where he belonged. The same as she'd be where she belonged.

As they rode along a ridge about three miles south of the Lonetree's headquarters, Brant pointed to the valley below. "What do you think of this?"

He heard Annie catch her breath. "Please make the horse stop."

With a slight pull of the reins, Dancer came to a halt. "What's wrong?"

She shook her head. "Nothing. I want to take a better look." She took off her sunglasses as she gazed down at the land below the low rise of the ridge. "I love the way pine trees ring the meadow on three sides and the stream winds from one end to the other." Turning to face him, she smiled. "This would be a wonderful place for a home."

Brant felt his chest tighten with feelings he'd rather not analyze as he gazed into her expressive green eyes. "That's exactly what I intend to do."

"Really?"

Grinning, he nodded. "I'm going to build the house and barns over there," he said, pointing to the east end of the valley. "And I'll have horses grazing over on the west side."

"That's the perfect place for it," she said, nodding. "But it has to be a certain kind of house."

His heart sank. Here it came. This was where she'd tell him about some modern-style brick-and-block structure that would look better on a golf course somewhere out East than in a hidden valley in Wyoming.

"What kind of home do you think would be best here?" he asked.

"It would definitely have to be a log home," she said, surprising him. "But different from the Lonetree ranch house. It would need lots of windows facing the west end of the valley, so you could see the sunset each evening." She paused thoughtfully. "The master bedroom should be on the second floor of that side, with glass doors leading out onto a balcony, too. That way you could sit outside in the summer and watch the sun as it slips behind the mountains."

Brant swallowed hard and the tightening in his chest turned to a warmth that invaded every cell in his body. Her description was exactly what he'd always envisioned. "You know, sweetpea, you're pretty damn amazing."

"Me?" She looked incredulous.

"Yes, you." Laughing, he hugged her close, and lowered his head to press a quick kiss to her soft, pink lips. "You've just managed to describe in less than five minutes what I've been planning for the last two years."

The realization that Annie wouldn't be sharing the house with him caused a pang of regret to twist his gut. But Brant pushed the feeling aside as he held her close and they gazed out across the valley that would one day be his home. She was in his arms now and that's all that mattered.

Seven

Two mornings after their ride up to his valley, Brant came downstairs feeling as if he'd been on a two-day bender. His head ached from lack of sleep, his insides burned and he felt as if he was about to jump out of his own skin.

He wanted Annie. It was as simple as that. And just as complicated.

He'd spent the last three nights tossing and turning, going over all the reasons why he shouldn't become involved with her—why kissing her, making love to her, would spell disaster. But his stubborn body wasn't listening to anything his head had to say. He'd taken more ice-cold showers since meeting Annie than he'd ever taken in his entire life. And after the initial shock wore off, nothing had changed. He still wanted her with a fierceness that scared the hell out of him.

For the past few days they'd played in the snow together like a couple of kids, he'd shown her around the Lonetree and taught her to ride a horse. And with each passing day, he watched a little more of the cautious, conservative Annie disappear, to be replaced by a confident, adventurous woman. A sexy as hell woman that he was finding it hard not to kiss, not to touch.

His body tightened and he gritted his teeth as he tried to get himself under control. They came from two different worlds, and past experience had taught him that her enjoyment of the western lifestyle was nothing more than a passing fancy. By the time he delivered her into her grandmother's care, she'd be ready to return to all that was familiar to her. She'd be tired of jeans and boots, of riding horses and looking at hidden valleys where a log house would someday stand.

He wandered into the kitchen expecting to find her sitting at the table having breakfast, but she wasn't there. He'd checked before coming downstairs and she wasn't in her room. Where could she be?

Walking through the great room, he headed for the foyer to see if her jacket was still hung on the pegs beside the front door. But glancing into the office, he stopped just past the doorway, then stepped back to take a better look. Annie sat in the desk chair, her attention fixed on the computer screen sitting on the stand to the left of the desk.

"Hey there, sweetpea," Brant said as he entered the room. "I wondered where you were."

Her smile made his knees weak and his pulse race. "I asked Morgan if I could use the computer to do an Internet search,'' she said, keying an address into the browser.

Rounding the desk, Brant stood behind her and glanced at the screen. ''What are you looking for?''

''I'm searching the archives of the newspapers in Fresno, California,'' she answered. ''When I first met Patrick, he mentioned that he'd lived and worked in the Fresno area before moving to Illinois.''

''What exactly are you looking for?'' he asked. ''Police reports?''

She nodded. ''Uh-huh.''

Annie looked so cute sitting there with her spun-gold hair tucked behind her ears, nibbling on her lower lip as she read what was on the screen. Brant wanted to pick her up and kiss her until they both needed oxygen. No matter how much he talked to himself and recounted all the reasons he should steer clear of her, he couldn't seem to keep his hands off her. Unable to resist, he lifted her hair to place a kiss at the nape of her neck.

''Is there anything I can do to help?'' he murmured against her satiny skin.

He felt a tiny shiver course through her a moment before she turned to smile up at him. ''As a matter of fact, there is something that you can do.''

''Name it, sweetpea.'' At that moment, if she'd asked him to go jump in the lake, he'd have found an ax, chopped a hole in the ice and dived in.

''Would you mind checking on your brother?'' she asked, her smile turning to a look of concern. ''He seemed really—'' she paused as if to think of a word to describe Morgan ''—I don't know. Sad?''

Brant glanced at the calendar on the desk and cursed his own shortsightedness. How could he have forgotten? "Today would have been Emily's thirty-first birthday."

"Emily?"

He nodded. "She was Morgan's fiancée."

"What happened?"

"She was killed a week before their wedding."

"Oh, how awful," Annie said, rising from the chair to wrap her arms around his shoulders. "You all must have loved her very much. How long has it been?"

"It will be five years this July." He took a deep breath against the tightening in his chest and hugged Annie close. They'd all cared for Emily and felt her loss deeply. But Brant hated seeing how much Morgan still suffered, how he still grieved her passing. "This date is always tough on Morgan because he proposed on her birthday and they set the date of their wedding that same night."

"Why don't you spend the day with him, Brant." Annie touched his cheek with her soft hand. "Maybe you could help him get his mind off his loss."

"You won't mind spending most of the day on your own?" he asked, feeling torn between wanting to help his brother and wanting to be with her.

She shook her head. "I'll be fine. I'm going to be busy looking through Internet files anyway." She rose on tiptoe to kiss his chin. "Besides, Morgan needs you right now."

"Did anybody ever tell you how special you are?" Brant asked, lowering his mouth to hers for a quick kiss.

Her lips beneath his caused an instant charge of electric current to streak through him and heat to surge through his veins. His lower body tightened instantly and he slid his hands from her waist to her hips. Drawing her close, he let her feel what she did to him, how she made him want her.

When her lips parted on a soft gasp, he took advantage of her reaction and slowly slipped inside to stroke the inner recesses of her mouth. Teasing, coaxing, he reveled in the sweet taste of her, the shy way she touched his tongue with hers.

She tangled her fingers in the hair brushing the collar of his chambray shirt, then slipped beneath to trace the column of his neck. The feel of her nails skimming across his skin caused his blood pressure to skyrocket and sent a surge of desire straight to the part of his anatomy that was already straining insistently against the fly of his jeans.

Brant broke the kiss and tried desperately to remember all the reasons why becoming involved with Annie would be a mistake. He couldn't think of a single one.

"Brant?" The sound of her passion-filled voice saying his name sent another wave of longing to every cell in his body.

Gazing down at the heightened color on her porcelain cheeks, he smiled. "You're about to kill me, Annie."

"Me?" She looked skeptical.

"Yes, you." He placed a kiss on the end of her cute little nose. "If you'll remember, I told you that I wasn't a gelding. That I'm a man with a man's desires. And right now, you're making me more aware of that fact than I've ever been in my life."

The blush on her cheeks deepened to almost the same shade of pink as her blouse, but the spark of desire in her green eyes brightened. He didn't think he'd ever seen a prettier sight. "I've never been the type of woman—"

He placed his finger to her lips and shook his head. "Sweetpea, I don't want to hear you say that about yourself again. The evidence that you *are* that type of woman is pressed up against you right now."

At Brant's heated look and candid statement, Annie's stomach did a backflip. Moistening her suddenly dry lips, she tried to think of something to say.

"Don't do that," he said, briefly closing his eyes.

"What?"

"Lick your lips," he said at the same time his body stirred against hers. He gazed at her. "It doesn't help my frame of mind right now."

Her eyes widened and her cheeks felt as if they were on fire. Averting her eyes to the front of his shirt, she murmured, "I...um, sorry."

Chuckling, Brant stepped back and she watched him take several deep breaths. "Sweetpea, don't be sorry. Just don't do it again when I'm in this kind of shape." He reached out to place his forefinger under her chin. Lifting her head until their gazes met, he smiled. "Otherwise, I might not be able to keep my promise."

"Your promise?"

He nodded. "I told you that you could trust me. But this gallantry stuff is taking its toll." Leaning down to whisper in her ear, he added, "There's nothing that I'd like more right now than to take you upstairs to my bed and make love to you for the rest of the day and night."

Before Annie could find her voice, he kissed her on the forehead and walked out of the office without a backward glance. Collapsing in the chair behind her, she stared off into space as she came to terms with what he'd said.

He wanted her. Brant Wakefield actually wanted her the way a man wants a woman.

She'd known he liked her, enjoyed showing her around the ranch and seemed to like kissing her. But he wanted to make love to her? That was going to take some getting used to. She'd never had a man tell her that she created *that* kind of passion in him.

Nibbling on her lower lip, she turned back to the computer but sat staring at the blinking cursor for a good ten minutes after Brant left the room. There was no doubt in her mind now that she'd fallen in love with him. He was the kindest, most generous man she'd ever met, and from the moment they met he'd made her feel protected and cherished. But could he love her in return?

He'd said he wanted her, but that wasn't the same as loving her. And although she was far from experienced in relationships between men and women, she had enough knowledge about the opposite sex to know that love wasn't a prerequisite for sleeping together.

A shiver ran the length of her spine. Beyond a few passionless kisses and a handful of clumsy hugs, Patrick had never shown that she excited him in any way. She shook her head. He'd shown more enthusiasm for her grandmother's bank accounts than he had for her. And other than a few dates in college, Annie didn't have a clue about passion and desire.

Taking a deep steadying breath, she decided it would be best to forget about what Brant had said and concentrate on searching the archives of the Fresno-area newspapers. It was much easier on her peace of mind to look for something to incriminate Patrick than to think about what was happening between herself and Brant.

Late that afternoon, Annie tucked her denim skirt around her feet as she curled up in one corner of the couch in front of the fireplace in the great room. Shuffling through the papers in her hands, she smiled. She'd found more than enough in Patrick's background to convince her grandmother to notify the authorities and start an investigation.

"What have you got there, sweetpea?" Brant asked, entering the room from the kitchen.

Glancing up, she watched his easy gait as he walked over to her. His jeans were worn and soft-looking, and they encased his long, muscular legs like a second skin. She swallowed hard and looked back down at the papers she held.

"I found—" When he sat down next to her on the big leather couch, he rested his arm along the back, then tangled his fingers in her hair. She had to clear her throat before she could finish. "I found out that Patrick was arrested for embezzlement seven years ago, then convicted and sentenced to five years in prison."

"Let me see." Brant reached for the printouts. His hand touched hers and a tiny little charge of electricity snaked up her arm.

"What he'd done wasn't discovered until after the elderly woman died and her children were dividing up the estate," Annie said, pointing to a passage on the page he held. "Since it was considered a white-collar crime, he served his sentence in a minimum-security facility."

"But, with your suspicions, this should be enough to start an investigation," Brant said, giving her a smile that curled her toes.

"Or at the very least, convince my grandmother to have her accounts audited," Annie said, nodding.

"You did good, sweetpea. Real good." He took the papers and laid them on the coffee table, then turned to pull her to him. "Why didn't you think of this before?"

The feel of his strong arms around her made thinking difficult. "I...I'm not sure why I didn't think to do an Internet search when I first suspected he was embezzling from Grandmother, but after you mentioned our going to Anaheim, I remembered that Patrick had come from California."

"And a leopard doesn't change its spots, does it?" Brant asked, grinning.

Smiling back, she shook her head. "I always thought it odd that he never wanted to talk about living there. Almost everyone wants to tell you where they came from and about their past accomplishments. But every time I asked, he'd change the subject."

Brant laughed. "It's my bet old pasty-face came right out of the California penal system just before he moved to your hometown."

She nodded. "I'm sure he probably did."

They sat staring at the fire for several long minutes before Annie broke the silence. "How's Morgan?"

"He'll be okay," Brant said, his arms tightening around her. "I talked him into riding down to Laramie with one of Colt's friends this evening. Jake Weston wants to look at a horse some guy has for sale down that way and Morgan has a good eye for horseflesh. Then, if I know Jake, he'll talk Morgan into stopping by Buffalo Gals in Bear Creek for a few beers on their way back.'' Brant chuckled. ''By the time Morgan gets home tonight, all he'll want to do is go to bed and sleep.''

''He'll get drunk?''

Smiling, Brant shook his head. ''Not really. If Morgan drinks more than three beers, all he wants to do is sleep.'' Brant nuzzled the side of her neck, sending a shiver up her spine. ''Just be glad his room is on the opposite end of the house.''

''Wh-why?'' she asked breathlessly.

''Because most of the night he'll be snoring so loud it'll sound like a freight train is barreling through.''

She laughed. ''Louder than you, huh?''

''I don't snore,'' he said, shaking his head.

''Yes, you do.''

''Nope.''

Before she could argue with him further, Brant ran his fingers up and down her ribs, sending her into a fit of laughter. ''St-stop,'' she gasped.

''What will you give me to stop?'' he asked, continuing to tickle her.

''A-anything,'' she said, squirming to put distance between them.

''How about a hug?''

''Y-yes.''

His fingers immediately stilled and it was then that Annie realized her squirming had landed her flat of her back on the couch. Stretching out beside her, Brant took her into his arms and stared down at her for what seemed an eternity before he spoke. ''Sweetpea, I've spent a miserable day.''

''You have?'' The simple act of breathing suddenly

took great effort and she wondered fleetingly whether it was from being tickled or from the proximity of the man holding her to his body.

He nodded. "I kept reminding myself of all the reasons why I should keep my hands off you."

She wondered if she'd ever get used to his outspokenness. "And did you reach any conclusions?" she asked, slightly shocked that she'd voiced the question. She really wasn't sure she wanted to know.

Shaking his head, he brushed her mouth with his. "All I was able to decide was that I want you like I've never wanted any other woman."

Every cell in her being tingled to life at Brant's admission. "I—I don't know what to say," she stammered.

"Tell me to leave you alone, Annie," he said, kissing her forehead, her cheeks. "Tell me to get the hell away from you and keep my hands to myself."

Heaven help her, but that was the very last thing she wanted. Shoring up her courage, she shook her head. "I can't do that, Brant."

Groaning, he buried his head in her hair. "Why, Annie? Why can't you tell me to leave you alone?"

"Because…" She took a deep breath. "Because I like it when you kiss me, when you touch me."

She felt his big body shudder against her before he raised his head to gaze down at her. "That's the problem, sweetpea. I like it, too. In fact, I like it so much, I don't think I can continue to be a gentleman and walk away the next time I kiss you."

His incredibly blue eyes pinned her with their intensity and she could see the turbulence in their depths, the war he was waging with himself. He wanted her, but if she told him that wasn't what she wanted, he would back off, no matter how difficult it was for him.

Closing her eyes for a moment to gather her courage, she opened them to meet his gaze head-on. "Kiss me, Brant."

"Dammit, Annie, didn't you hear what I said?" he asked, his arms tightening around her. "If I kiss you, I won't be able to walk away this time. I'll keep on kissing you until one thing leads to another and I make love to you."

"I don't want you to walk away," she said, reaching up to place her hand at the back of his head. Drawing his head down, she touched her lips to his. "I want you to stay right here and kiss me, touch me…" She paused, then feeling as if she were jumping off a cliff, she finished, "…make love to me."

A groan rumbled up from deep in his chest a moment before his mouth came down on hers. At the first contact of his lips, Annie's eyes drifted shut and she felt as if lightning skipped over every nerve in her body. A warmth like she'd never known began to flow though her and she wrapped her arms around his broad shoulders as he traced her mouth with his strong tongue.

When he pressed forward to enter her mouth, he ran his hand down her side to tug her blouse from the waistband of her denim skirt. The feel of his palm at her waist, the contrast of a callused masculine hand as it skimmed over smooth feminine skin sent her temperature soaring and a shimmer of excitement snaking down her spine. But when his hand cupped the underside of her breast, Annie moaned and clutched his shoulders.

Breaking the kiss, Brant chafed her nipple through

the lace of her bra as he nibbled his way to the sensitive hollow behind her ear. "Does that feel good, sweetpea?"

"Y-yes."

He raised his head to gaze down at her. "Are you sure you want to make love with me, Annie?"

She nodded. "I've never been more sure of anything in my life, Brant."

He pulled his hand from beneath her blouse, then touching her cheek with his index finger, he drew it down to trace her lower lip. He stared at her for what seemed an eternity and the heat in his dark blue eyes took her breath.

Slowly rising from the couch, he held his hand out to her. "Let's go upstairs, sweetpea."

When Annie trustingly placed her hand in his, Brant felt as if he'd been handed a rare gift. Pulling her up to stand beside him, his heart pounded against his rib cage and his body tightened with need. They were about to take a step that would change everything between them.

"Are you really sure about this, Annie?" he asked again. The last thing he wanted was her having regrets in the morning about what they would share tonight.

To his immense relief, she nodded. "There's not a doubt in my mind, Brant."

Relieved beyond words to hear that she wanted him as much as he wanted her, he led her over to the staircase, wrapped his arm around her waist and together they climbed the stairs and walked down the hall to his room. Closing the door behind them, Brant switched on the bedside lamp.

"Brant?"

He turned to face her and the shy smile curving her

perfect lips sent his blood pressure up several points. "What, sweetpea?"

"There's…um, something I think you should know." She nervously nibbled on her lower lip as she gazed up at him.

"And what would that be?" he asked, pulling her into his arms. He lowered his head to bury his face in the silky strands of her herbal-scented hair. "If you're worried about protection. Don't. I'll take care of everything."

"Oh, I hadn't thought of that," she said, wrapping her arms around his waist. "Thank you, but that's not what I need to tell you."

A tingle of apprehension streaked up his spine. "What exactly do you need to tell me, Annie?"

She kissed the skin at the exposed vee of his shirt, sending a wave of heat straight to his loins. "I might not be very good at this. And you may even have to tell me what to do at times."

He swallowed hard as he tried to get his suddenly dry throat to work.

But before he could vocalize his thoughts, she confirmed his suspicion. "I've never done this before," she whispered.

Eight

Brant suddenly felt as if he'd run headfirst into a brick wall. He pulled back to gaze at her. ''Never?''

She shook her head.

Swallowing hard, he released her, took a step back, then another. He ran a shaky hand over the sudden tension gripping his neck and took a deep breath. ''You're a virgin.''

''That's usually the case when someone has never made love,'' she said, nodding.

''And you want me to be the first man you make love with?''

''Yes,'' she said, sounding about as certain as anyone he'd ever heard.

''Why, Annie?'' He blew out the air trapped in his lungs as he tried to focus on all the reasons he should send her to her room, while he jumped into an ice-cold shower and stayed there until he spit ice cubes. "Why me? Why now?"

She closed the distance between them. "Because you're kind, giving, and, the sexiest man I've ever met." Reaching out, she took his hand in hers. "And you've made me feel more like a real woman in the last few days than I've ever felt in my life."

The touch of her soft skin on his callused palm, the look of pure desire in her expressive green eyes and the smile curving her sensuous lips caused blood to surge through his veins with a force that made him light-headed. He closed his eyes in an effort to think clearly. But the feel of her fingers skimming over his knuckles, the pads of her fingertips as they traced a slow line up to the erratic pulse at his wrist, was playing hell with his reasoning.

"That's not all," she said, her sweet voice flowing over him like a warm caress.

He opened his eyes. "There…" He had to stop to clear the rust from his throat. "There's more?"

Nodding, she gave him a smile that sent his good intentions right out the window. "I want to be close to you in every way a woman can be close to a man. I want to be part of you, and you part of me."

Groaning, Brant pulled her back into his arms and held her close. "Dammit, woman, you aren't going to make this easy, are you?" He took a deep shuddering breath, then stared down at her. "You have no idea how much I want to hold you in my arms and bury myself deep inside you. But if I do that, I'll be taking something from you that you can never get back."

"I know."

"And I'd rather die than have you regret one minute—"

She placed her index finger to his mouth, stopping the rest of his argument. "The only regret I'll have is if we don't make love, Brant."

He kissed her finger. "But, sweetpea, you need to understand. I can't make any promises—"

"I'm not asking for any," she said, interrupting him. "It's my choice." Her smile made his mouth go dry. "I want you to be the first man to touch me."

And I'd damn well better be the only man to touch you.

The thought stopped him short. But as he gazed into Annie's luminous green eyes, Brant knew in his soul it was true. He did want to be the only man to hold her, touch her, make love to her. He swallowed hard and ignored the disturbing realization. If he thought too much about it, he was afraid he'd discover something about himself he wasn't yet ready to face.

He closed his eyes again and tried to fight what he was beginning to realize was a losing battle. With Annie's arms wrapped around his waist, her head nestled trustingly against his chest, there was no way in hell he could be noble and send her to her room. He was going to make love to her.

"Sweetpea, I…" Brant forgot what he was about to say as a sudden thought sent a chill straight through him. "I don't want to hurt you."

Stepping back, she reached up to unfasten the first snap on his chambray shirt. "Brant, I know there's going to be some discomfort." She moved down to the second snap. "But I trust you. I know you'll be gentle."

The feel of her fingers on his skin as she released the snap closures on his shirt had Brant clenching his back teeth so hard, he was sure they'd crack under the pressure. He took one deep breath, then another as he fought to control the sudden surge of need flowing through his veins. Annie was putting her faith and trust in him to make her first time as easy as possible. And he'd walk through hell and back to see that her confidence in him wasn't misplaced.

"I promise you that I'll do everything I can to make this easy for you, sweetpea," he said, taking her hands in his. He kissed her fingertips. "But you're going to have to help me."

"How?"

"You're going to have to stop touching me for just a few minutes," he said, trying to force his lungs to take in some much-needed air. He grinned at her puzzled expression. "Otherwise, I'm going to set the house on fire."

She smiled back at him. "That wouldn't be a good idea. It's freezing outside."

He groaned and shook his head. "I've already been frozen enough in the last few days to last me a lifetime." Seeing the question in her expressive gaze, he chuckled. "I've been taking cold showers ever since we rented that motel room in Denver."

"Really?" She looked surprised.

He brushed a strand of silky blond hair from her smooth cheek. "You have no idea how sexy you are, do you, sweetpea?"

"I...I've never thought of myself that way," she said, her sweet voice breathless.

Brant unbuttoned the top button of her red calico blouse, then smiling, lowered his head to kiss the exposed skin along her collarbone as he eased the second button through its opening. ''Believe me, you've got more sex appeal in your little finger than most women have in their whole body.'' He smiled when she shivered beneath his lips.

Raising his head, he held her gaze as he worked the next couple of buttons through their holes. He let the backs of his fingers brush the smooth skin of her abdomen, and by the time he reached the waistband of her denim skirt, he wasn't sure which one of them was breathing harder. When he pulled the tail of her blouse loose and parted the garment, his heart slammed against his chest at the sight of her red, lacy see-through bra.

''Is this one of the items you bought in that lingerie place in the mall in Denver?'' he asked, his voice cracking like a teenager's.

''Yes,'' she said, treating him to a smile that spiked his blood pressure by a good fifty points. ''I buy all of my underthings from the Sleek and Sassy Lady Lingerie Boutiques.''

Brant ran his finger along the edge of one lacy cup. ''I think I love that store,'' he said, blowing out a pent-up breath.

''I've heard a lot of men like looking at their catalogs,'' she said, her throaty laughter sending a streak of longing straight to his groin.

He pushed her blouse from her shoulders and down her arms. ''The real thing is a whole lot better than seeing it in a catalog.''

Tossing the cotton shirt on the trunk at the end of his bed, he reached behind her to unhook the back closure, then pull the tiny straps from her arms. The sight of her full perfect breasts caused his body to throb and his hands to shake slightly when he reached up to fill his palms with her creamy softness.

"You're beautiful, Annie."

At the feel of hard male calluses cupping her smooth feminine skin, Annie felt as if she'd melt into a puddle at his big, booted feet. But when he chafed her nipples with the pads of his thumbs, ribbons of heated excitement threaded their way from every part of her to gather into a swirling coil in the pit of her stomach. Reaching out, she grasped Brant's biceps to steady herself.

"Does that feel good, sweetpea?"

His smile, the desire in his deep blue gaze and the sound of his voice rough with passion spread heat throughout her entire body. Catching her lower lip between her teeth, she tried desperately to keep a moan from escaping.

"Don't hide it, Annie," he said, leaning forward to whisper close to her ear. "Let me hear you when it feels good."

If she could have formed words, Annie would have told him that she was pretty sure proper ladies weren't supposed to moan. But when he lowered his head and took one taut bud into his mouth, she felt more like a real woman and less like a proper lady with each passing second. The tip of his tongue flicking her sensitized flesh, the moist heat of his mouth and his gentle sucking tightened the coil in her belly and made stifling the sound of her growing desire impossible.

When Brant raised his head, his slow, sexy smile made her knees wobble. "That's it, sweetpea. Let me know I'm bringing you pleasure."

"It's not fair," she said raggedly. "I want to touch you, too."

She reached up to take hold of the lapels of his shirt, then gave one quick jerk. Every snap on the blue chambray popped open, revealing Brant's well-developed chest and stomach.

"You're gorgeous," she said, placing her palms on the rise of his pectoral muscles.

He chuckled. "I've been called a lot of things. But gorgeous is a first."

Exploring the hard sinew, she traced her index finger around his flat nipples. The flesh puckered, and at his low groan, she glanced up. "Does that feel as good for me to touch you as it does for you to touch me?"

"Sweetpea, if it felt any better I doubt that I could stand it," he said, quickly shrugging out of his shirt.

He pulled her into his arms and the feel of his bare skin against hers, the beating of his heart keeping time with her own, tightened the coil in her stomach and sent tiny charges of electricity skipping over every nerve ending in her body. As his lips nibbled the hollow behind her ear and the side of her neck, Annie wrapped her arms around him. Splaying her hands across his broad back, she clung to him as wave after wave of heated sensation swept through her.

As he held her to him, Annie felt his hands slip between them to release the button at the waistband of her skirt, then slide the zipper down. Stepping back, he smiled encouragingly as he gave a little tug and the denim fell to her feet. When his gaze drifted down her body, she heard his sharp intake of breath, saw his body shudder at the sight of her red garter belt and matching red thong.

She watched him close his eyes and breathe deeply for several long seconds before he spoke. "Annie, I swear you're going to give me a heart attack with your choice of underwear.'' His voice sounded deeper than it had only moments before.

"You don't like what I'm wearing?" she teased.

His eyes popped open and the hunger she saw in the deep blue depths took her breath. "I love what you have on, sweetpea," he said, grinning. He ran his index finger along one of the garters. "But I think I'm going to love taking these little wisps of lace off you even more.''

Annie barely managed to stand still as Brant unhooked the garters from the tops of her hose, then slowly pulled the nylons down her legs, caressing her thighs, her calves and the arch of her foot as he went. Straightening, he ran his hands beneath the elastic band of her garter belt and in one quick motion swept it from her body.

Pulling her to him, he nuzzled the side of her neck as he ran his hands down her back to cup her bottom and draw her closer. Shivers of need raced through her when he hooked his thumbs in the tiny waistband at the back of her thong, then pulled it down to fall at her feet.

He stepped away from her then, and the appreciation in his fiery gaze made her heart skip a beat. "You're beautiful, Annie," he said, his voice so reverent there wasn't a doubt in her mind that he meant it.

Nibbling on her lower lip, Annie gathered her courage, and reached out to trace her finger along the line of dark hair arrowing down from his navel to disappear below his belt buckle. "I like the way you look in jeans, Brant. But I'd like to see you out of them.''

His stomach quivered as she worked the leather

belt strap through the metal buckle, then popped the snap at his waistband. "May I?" she asked, glancing up at him.

"Aw, hell, sweetpea, I'll be disappointed if you don't," he said, grinning.

She smiled back, then taking the tab between her thumb and index finger, eased the zipper down. Her hand brushed the hard ridge of his arousal straining at his white cotton briefs and a shiver of feminine power coursed through her. But when she started to push his jeans from his lean hips, Brant caught her hands in his.

"I think I'd better take care of the rest of this," he said, sounding as out of breath as she felt.

Annie stood mesmerized as Brant removed his boots, jeans and briefs. She'd never seen a nude man, unless she counted the statues and nude artwork in museums. But the simple act of watching Brant disrobe had a far different effect on her than any work of art. Her heart was racing and the room suddenly seemed to be devoid of oxygen.

He removed something from the pocket of his jeans and placed it under one of the pillows, then turned to face her. Annie's heart skipped several beats and her eyes widened. Brant was, in a word, gorgeous. His body was far from average and looked as if it had been sculpted with an artist's eye for detail. His shoulders were wide, his chest and stomach muscles well defined, his hips and flanks lean. Long muscular legs carried him toward her, but the sight of his impressive arousal caused her heart to stop completely, then take off at a gallop. She didn't have any prior experience to draw from, but something told her that Brant was above average in more than one way.

Her gaze flew to his. He was looking at her as if she was the most desirable woman on earth. "It's all right, sweetpea," he said, catching her hands in his. "I promise we'll fit just fine."

Brant led Annie to the side of the bed, then pulling back the comforter and sheet, picked her up to gently place her on the soft flannel sheets. Stretching out beside her, he gathered her into his arms. He loved the feel of her small body against his, the contrast of soft curvy female to hard angular male.

But the feel of her warmth pressed to him quickly had Brant grinding his teeth and praying for the strength to take things slow. He'd never been so turned on in his life, and they'd barely gotten their clothes off.

Propping himself on one elbow, he leaned over to stare down at her. "Sweetpea, we're going to take this slow and easy," he said, feeling the need to reassure her.

But apparently Annie meant what she'd said when she told him that she trusted him, because she wrapped her arms around his neck, pulled his head down to hers and planted a kiss on him that made him feel as if he just might go up in a blaze of glory. Her perfect lips on his, the shy way she deepened the kiss, sent a wave of longing straight through him and had his body throbbing with the need to brand her as his.

When she finally let him up for air, he shook his head. "Damn, woman, you're about to kill me." He pressed his lips to the slope of her breasts, then nibbling his way to the hardened tip, he added, "And I'm loving every minute of it."

He felt her slender fingers thread through his hair

and hold him to her as he teased the tight bud. "Brant…I think…you're the one…killing me."

Brant grinned and raised his head. "Want me to stop, sweetpea?"

She gave him a shy smile, then closed her eyes. "No."

Kissing her sweet lips, he ran his hand over her ribs to her trim waist. "Your skin is so smooth. Just like a piece of fine satin." He felt her shiver against him when he continued the exploration over the curve of her hip and down her outer thigh. "Annie?"

"Mmm?"

"Look at me."

When her eyelids fluttered open, he held her gaze as he moved his hand to brush the inner part of her thigh. "I want you to promise me something."

"At this point…I'll promise you…anything," she said, her hands tightening on his shoulders as he drew closer to her feminine secrets.

"Tell me what feels good," he said, touching her at the juncture of her thighs.

Parting her, Brant found her moist heat, stroked the tiny pleasure point with the pad of his thumb. "I…please…" Her voice trailed off into a soft moan.

He watched her close her eyes and a blush of desire begin to color her porcelain cheeks. "Please what?"

"Please…do something," she whispered, moving restlessly against him.

"What do you want me to do?" he asked, continuing to tease her.

Her eyes flew open and she met his gaze head-on. "Make love…to me, Brant. Now."

Her throaty demand sent blood surging through his veins, but when he dipped his finger into her honeyed warmth to test her, Brant was the one having to take several deep breaths to slow his own libido. Her complete readiness for him almost sent him over the edge. She wanted him as badly as he wanted her.

"Just a minute, sweetpea," he said, retrieving a foil packet from beneath the pillow with a shaky hand.

After arranging their protection, Brant gathered her into his arms and kissed her as he parted her legs with his knee. When he broke the kiss, their gazes locked and he moved to cover her small body with his. Neither one of them spoke as he found her and moved himself into the tight warmth of her luscious body.

His body urged him to plunge forward, to bury himself deep inside her, but he held back. Annie was new to making love, and her body needed time to adjust to the invasion of his.

The strain of holding himself back caused Brant's muscles to quiver and burn as he carefully eased forward. Watchful for any sign of discomfort, he stopped when he reached the barrier of her virginity.

"Annie," was all he could manage to say a moment before he covered her mouth with his, and kissing her, pushed past the veil to make her his own.

Brant felt her soft gasp against his lips, her nails scoring his shoulders as he merged them into one. Being inside of Annie was heaven and hell rolled into one. The thought that he'd caused her any kind of pain just about tore him apart, yet his body was urging him to complete their union, to race toward the summit of mind-shattering completion. But Annie wasn't ready for that and he'd die before he hurt her any more than he'd already done.

Holding his body perfectly still, he raised his head

and brushed a strand of silky blond hair from her forehead. "I'm sor—"

"Brant, it's all right," she said, smiling and placing her finger to his lips to stop his apology. Even as she spoke, he felt her body relaxing around his, accepting him as part of her.

When she arched into him, Brant had to concentrate on the control he was trying so hard to maintain. Annie was telling him without words that she was ready for the next step in their lovemaking, that she wanted him to take her to a place only lovers go. He answered her movement as he slowly, carefully began to move inside her.

He watched the passion once again color her cheeks, felt her body fully accept his. His muscles burned with the need to quicken the pace, to race to the satisfaction that awaited him. But he fought it. Brant was determined to bring Annie to the brink with him, to make sure she too found release from the sizzling tension surrounding them.

Easing his hand between them, he gently stroked her and reveled in the urgent need widening her pretty, green eyes, the tightening of her body around his. He sensed that she was close, and leaning forward, whispered against her lips, "Let go, sweetpea. I'll take care of you."

He watched Annie tightly close her eyes, then heard her moan his name as she gave in to the storm of pleasure raging within her. Tiny feminine muscles clutched at him and he felt himself being drawn into the tempest with her. But only after he was sure her passion was spent did he submit to his own hungry need.

Groaning her name, Brant wrapped both arms

around her and held her close as he thrust into her one final time. A charge of electric current seemed to course through him a moment before his body stiffened, then spasmed as he found his own release.

Annie held Brant close as his big body shuddered, then sagged on top of her. She loved the feel of his weight pressing her into the mattress, loved the way his harsh breathing felt against the sensitive skin of her neck as he recovered from their lovemaking.

She squeezed her eyes shut and caught her lower lip between her teeth. She might as well face facts. She loved everything about Brant. And the fact that their time together was fast approaching an end was almost more than she could bear. Tomorrow they would leave for Anaheim, then two days later go to her home in Illinois.

"Are you all right?" he asked. His lips moving against her skin sent shivers of renewed excitement up her spine.

"I'm wonderful," she said, hugging him tighter.

He propped himself on one forearm to gaze down at her, and the concern on his handsome face took her breath. "Are you sure, sweetpea?"

Smiling, she nodded. "That was the most incredible experience of my life."

He stared at her for several long seconds before his charming grin broke through. "I promise that next time it will be even better."

Her heart skipped a beat and her stomach fluttered. "Next time?"

"Oh, yeah, sweetpea." He moved to her side, gathered her into his arms and pulled the sheet and comforter over them. "But not tonight."

"Why not?" She immediately felt her cheeks heat

with embarrassment at the disappointment she detected in her own voice.

Brant cupped her breast with one large hand and kissed her shoulder. "I hated having to hurt you in order to make love to you, sweetpea. And I don't intend for it to happen again."

"It wasn't—"

"I don't want you getting sore," he said, shaking his head.

Annie felt his lower body stir against her. "But—"

He took a deep breath and hugged her close. "We'll wait."

She'd started to tell him that it hadn't been *that* uncomfortable. But the gentleness of his tone, the protective way he held her, took her breath. Brant was trying to do what he thought was best for *her,* not what he really wanted to do. She'd never felt more cherished in her entire life.

Long after his soft snores signaled that he'd fallen asleep, Annie lay within Brant's warm embrace, staring at the ceiling. In a few days, she'd be back home presenting her grandmother with evidence that Patrick Elsworth was a crook and hopefully convince the woman to have her accounts audited.

So why did the prospect of completing what she'd set out to do leave her feeling so…empty?

Turning her head to gaze at Brant's handsome features relaxed in sleep, Annie wondered if he would try to stay in contact with her after he took her to her grandmother's. Or would he leave her behind and never look back?

A lump formed in her throat and tears filled her eyes. She knew exactly why she felt the way she did. Returning to Illinois meant that she might never again be with the only man she'd ever loved.

Nine

Brant paid the cabdriver, then turned to take Annie by the elbow to guide her toward the personnel entrance of the arena in Anaheim. He'd purposely avoided thinking about this day. But now that it was here, there was no way to avoid it.

After the last round of the PBR event ended this evening, he and Annie would board a plane to Saint Louis, then rent a car and drive to her home in southern Illinois. The first thing tomorrow morning, she'd be back to her life of books, art and charity functions, and he'd return to the Lonetree and the unpretentious life he loved.

It's the way things were meant to be. The way they had to be. But if that was the case, why did his gut clench into a tight knot every time he thought about it?

When they entered the building and walked down

a long corridor into an open area, they sidestepped a man wearing headphones as he danced across the floor. "I know that different people have their own ways of preparing for these things," Annie said, looking doubtful. "But break dancing?"

Putting his disturbing thoughts aside, Brant laughed. "That's Gil Daniels, the barrelman. He's practicing."

"I remember seeing him in Saint Louis, but we weren't introduced," she said as Gil did a couple of backspins, then moonwalked his way to the other side of the staging area. "By the way, what does he do besides dance and hide in the barrel when the bull gets too close?"

"A barrelman distracts the bull occasionally, but mostly he entertains the crowd between rides and while the bulls are loaded into the chutes," Brant answered, steering her down the corridor leading to the VIP area.

"It doesn't seem fair that you don't have a barrel to jump into when the bull chases you," she said, sounding concerned.

"Don't worry about me," he said, chuckling. "I'm pretty quick on my feet."

Looking down at the sexiest woman he'd ever known, his smile faded. How was he ever going to be able to let her go?

Night before last, he'd made love to her for the first time. But due to a flight delay yesterday, they'd had to rush straight from the airport to the arena in order to make it to last night's round of bull riding. Then, by the time they got checked into the hotel, Annie had been so tired, she'd fallen asleep almost as soon as her head hit the pillow.

But Brant couldn't bear the thought of not holding her one more time, making love to her.

"Annie?"

"What?"

"I have something to ask you," he said, making a snap decision.

He stopped, set his duffel bag down and took her into his arms. God, how he loved touching her, holding her soft little body to his.

"Would you mind—"

"Tell him to stay on his toes today, Annie," Colt said as he and his best friend, Mitch Simpson, along with a crowd of other riders and their families, walked toward them. Both men stopped, gave Brant a knowing grin and a thumbs-up. "I've got a rematch with Kamikaze this evening."

"Try landing on your feet instead of your head and I won't have to worry about saving your sorry behind," Brant retorted, irritated by the interruption.

Both men laughed as Mitch stuck out his hand to Annie. Brant reluctantly loosened his hold on her but kept his arm around her shoulders and held her to his side.

"I don't think we've been introduced. I'm Mitch Simpson. I think you sat with my kid sister in Saint Louis."

Annie placed her hand in Mitch's, and Brant clenched his back teeth together so hard he figured it would take a crowbar to pry them apart. Mitch had a reputation with the ladies, rivaled only by Colt's, and Brant was having a hell of a time resisting the urge to belt the man.

"I'm Annie Devereaux," she said, smiling. "I enjoyed talking with Kaylee. But I didn't see her last night. Will she be here today?''

"No," Mitch said, continuing to hold Annie's hand. "She stayed home to coddle that new mare I bought her for her birthday."

"Tell her I'm sorry I didn't get to see her," Annie said.

When Brant sent a dark scowl Mitch's way, the red-haired cowboy finally dropped Annie's hand, but the grin he sent Brant's way was anything but repentant. "Kaylee said the two of you had a good time. She's going to be sorry she missed you, too."

"Yeah, can you believe that?" Colt asked, grinning. "She'd rather spend time with that buckskin nag than watch me ride."

Brant studied Colt. Was that a hint of disappointment he heard in his brother's voice?

"Kaylee's got more sense than to waste her time watching the likes of you," Mitch teased. "She's seen you ride enough to know what's going to happen."

"What's wrong with the way I ride?" Colt asked with mock indignation.

"It's not your ride," Mitch said, laughing. "It's your dismount. You always land on your head and they end up carrying you out of the arena, toes up."

"Do not," Colt said stubbornly.

"Do too," Mitch insisted.

The two men tipped their Resistols to Annie and continued the good-natured ribbing as they walked on toward the VIP area where the buffet tables had been set up.

Turning his attention back to Annie, Brant wrapped

his arms around her again. "Now, let's get back to what I wanted to ask you."

She smiled at him and he felt warm all the way to the darkest corners of his soul. "Ask away, cowboy."

"I've already checked us out of the hotel, but would you mind if I got another room somewhere and changed our flight to sometime tomorrow?" he asked, his request spilling out in a rush.

Her smile faded and for several long, wordless seconds, she stared at him. "Are you asking me to spend one more night with you, Brant?" she finally asked softly.

"Yes."

Placing her hand to his cheek, she nodded. "I'd like that." She nibbled on her lower lip for a moment before she added, "I want to spend one more night with you holding me, making love to me." She looked thoughtful for a moment before smiling shyly. "Besides, you made me a promise you haven't kept."

"I did?" With the sweet sound of her voice wrapping around him, the feel of her body close to his, he could barely remember his own name.

Rising on tiptoe, she whispered close to his ear, "You promised that when we made love again, it would be even more incredible than the first time." She kissed his chin, then smiled. "But we haven't made love again. So you owe me, cowboy."

His heart slammed against his ribs and his body immediately jerked to life. Here they stood in the middle of a crowd and he was getting harder than hell just thinking about holding her, loving her.

Brant grinned. "Sweetpea, I'm a man of my word. I'll change our airline reservations right after we grab a bite to eat."

After dining with the bull riders and other PBR personnel in the VIP room, Annie stood behind the bucking shoots, waiting for Brant to return from changing into his bullfighting garb. As she watched the men preparing the dirt floor in the arena, she thought about how eagerly she'd accepted Brant's invitation to delay their trip home by another day.

Carlotta Whittmeyer's very dutiful, prim-and-proper granddaughter, Anastasia, would never dream of telling a man that she'd like to spend the night making love with him. But a week ago, Anastasia had taken a chance, walked along a ledge and changed her life forever. And with the encouragement of a kind, caring, sexy cowboy, she'd become Annie—a woman who was beginning to learn the joy of experiencing life, not just watching it pass her by.

Smiling, Annie glanced down at her clothes. Even they were different. Anastasia preferred loose-fitting skirts and blouses in neutral, nondescript colors. She'd never dream of wearing a bright red, tapered shirt, formfitting jeans and western boots. But Annie found that she really liked them. She liked the colors, the way they felt, and the way Brant looked at her when she wore them. Reaching up, she grinned as she touched the wide brim of her black Resistol. She even liked wearing a western hat.

Unfortunately, her grandmother would never embrace the change in her. Sighing, Annie stared at the brightly colored, padded barrel waiting to be rolled out into the arena. Carlotta would expect Annie to be the same unadventurous creature who wore baggy clothes and lived life through the pages of a book.

But she could never be that person again. Nor could she dutifully follow her grandmother's directives. Annie was her own person now. And no matter what happened between herself and Brant, she would always be grateful to him for encouraging her to break free of that restrictive, narrow existence.

Lost in thoughts of how much she'd changed in the past week, it took a moment for the sound of a familiar male voice to catch her attention. But when it did, Annie froze. Afraid to move, she cast her gaze around to see where Patrick was. He had to be close. His voice was too clear, too loud, not to be more than a few feet away.

When she finally located him, her heart hammered in her chest. No more than ten feet to her left, Patrick stood with his back to her, talking to a group of cowboys. It appeared he was showing her picture to them and questioning them about seeing her.

Panic rose in her throat and she desperately looked around for somewhere to hide. Glancing to her right, she abandoned that direction immediately. There was no way she'd climb into an enclosure with one bull, let alone a pen filled with the large, mean-looking beasts. She'd rather take her chances with Patrick Elsworth than do that.

Think, Annie. Where was she going to go?

Her desperate gaze suddenly zeroed in on the barrel in front of her. It was big enough, and chances were, no one would think to look for her there.

Slowly, so as not to draw attention to herself, Annie eased up to the side of the specially made barrel, hoisted herself up and slipped inside. Holding her breath, she waited to see if Patrick had noticed.

But as the seconds ticked by, Annie began to relax. She'd wait a few more minutes, then climb out of the barrel and find Brant.

Just as she decided that Patrick had probably moved on and it was safe to leave her hiding place, she felt the barrel tilt precariously, then land on its side nearly knocking the breath from her. Feeling herself being rolled forward, she wondered what on earth was going on.

Then she realized exactly what was happening. Once the grounds crew finished preparing the dirt floor, the barrel would be moved into place. She was about to be rolled into the arena.

"Hey, stop! I'm in here!"

Unfolding her arm from where she had wrapped it around her waist in the close confines, Annie stretched it toward the opening to catch the attention of whoever was moving the barrel. Unable to see anything as she tumbled over and over, she blindly felt around until her fingers came into contact with a man's hand.

"What the hell?" the man shouted. The barrel was suddenly jerked upright and a very shocked-looking clown with an exaggerated greasepaint smile peered down at her through the opening. "Lady, what do you think you're doin' in there?"

"Please, keep your voice down," Annie pleaded. If Patrick was still in the vicinity, she didn't want the man giving her away. "I need you to find Brant Wakefield."

The man looked exasperated. "You need me to do what?"

Why did some men have to be so obtuse? She closed her eyes to the dizziness swirling within her from being rolled over and over, and tried to focus on being patient.

"Please, it's very important." When the man continued to stare down at her, anger cleared the last traces of her disorientation. "I'm not going to get out of your stupid barrel until you find Brant Wakefield. Is that clear enough for you?"

Brant looked at the crowd of people milling around the staging area. Where the hell was Annie? Fifteen minutes ago she'd been standing by the chutes watching the grounds crew level the dirt on the arena floor. Now she was nowhere in sight.

Seeing his brother walking toward him, Brant asked, "Have you seen Annie?"

Colt shook his head. "The last time I saw her was in the VIP room with you." He grinned. "Come to think of it, I haven't seen Mitch, either." At Brant's succinct curse, Colt's expression sobered. "Hey, I was just kidding. You know Mitch wouldn't beat your time with a woman."

"I know," Brant said, distracted.

Looking concerned, Colt asked, "Is something wrong?"

"I'm not sure," Brant said, continuing to scan the crowd.

"If you need help, you know all you have to do is say the word," Colt said seriously.

Brant nodded. "Thanks, Colt. I'll do that."

He watched his brother's relaxed stride carry him toward the back of the chutes where the rest of the riders were gathering. The one thing Brant had never doubted about his brothers was their loyalty, or their willingness to be there for him when the chips were down.

"Hey, Brant," Gil Daniels called. He hurried over

to where Brant stood. "I need your help with somethin'."

"Not now, Gil," Brant said, dismissing the man.

"This can't wait."

"It'll have to," Brant said impatiently. "I need to find someone."

When he started to walk away, Gil caught him by the arm. "You *need* to come with me."

Brant glared at the man. "I can't take the time right now, Gil. I've got to—"

"And I don't have time to wait for that little blonde you were with earlier to decide to get out of my barrel if you don't," Gil retorted.

"Annie's in the barrel?" Brant asked incredulously.

Gil shrugged and turned toward the barrel by the gate leading into the arena. "Hey, she didn't tell me her name and I didn't ask. All I know is she said she wouldn't get out of the damn thing until I found you."

Hurrying over to the barrel, Brant looked inside to find Annie gazing up at him. "What the hell are you doing in there?"

"Patrick's here."

"Are you sure?" he asked, looking around.

She nodded. "He was talking to some of the riders and showing them my picture."

He looked around. Elsworth was nowhere in sight. "He's gone now." Reaching his hand inside the opening, he helped Annie stand up, then lifted her from the barrel. "Sweetpea, you just about gave me a heart attack when Gil said you were inside this thing."

"She was about two seconds from being rolled out

into the arena,'' Gil grumbled as he once again tipped the barrel on its side and rolled it through the gate.

Brant watched Annie nervously nibble on her lower lip. ''It was the only place I could find to hide without Patrick seeing me.'' She shuddered. ''He was so close.''

Pulling her into his arms, Brant held her tightly. What the hell was he going to do to keep her safe? There were forty-five bull riders counting on him to be there to save their butts when they dismounted their rides. But the woman in his arms needed him to keep her safe from a far greater threat.

When he saw the event coordinator walking toward them, Brant breathed a sigh of relief. ''Sarah, I need your help.''

The tall, slender blond grinned. ''If it involves another shopping trip, it will have to wait until tomorrow.''

''Not this time,'' he said, shaking his head. Without going into a lot of detail, Brant explained that Annie was trying to avoid Elsworth. ''Can you keep Annie with you until the last round is over?''

''Of course.'' Sarah motioned for Annie to follow her. ''Come on, Annie. The guy you're trying to avoid won't be allowed behind the chutes. And if he does manage to find a way back there, we'll have forty-five cowboys with enough adrenaline running through their veins to take out a platoon of marines waiting for him.''

''Stay with Sarah,'' Brant said, kissing Annie on the forehead. ''I'll see you after the last ride.''

''Please be careful.''

''You can count on it, sweetpea.'' He grinned, and

lowering his voice so only she would hear, he added, "We have a date tonight."

He watched Annie follow Sarah, then hearing his name come across the loudspeaker, Brant turned to jog into the arena. He had no intention of letting a ton of pissed-off beef, a pasty-faced little weasel named Elsworth, or anything else stop him from spending the night with the most exciting woman he'd ever known.

Brant crouched in the ready position, waiting for the gateman to pull the rope and release the last ride of the night. In a split second, a rider astride two thousand pounds of bovine fury would explode from the chute and into the arena. Eight seconds after that, he'd make sure the cowboy made it to safety and his job would be done until next weekend.

When the gate swung wide, Brant waited a moment then ran in front of the bull. Circling close, he successfully turned it and kept the animal from carrying the rider too far out into the arena and a safe getaway.

But four seconds into the ride, the cowboy lost his grasp on the bull rope and fell to the ground dangerously near the bull's heavy hooves. When the rider failed to move, Brant knew immediately that the man had been knocked unconscious from hitting the ground headfirst. Without hesitation, he fell on top of the cowboy, covering the defenseless man with his own body, protecting him from the pounding Brant knew the bull was famous for giving to fallen riders. He'd never lost a rider yet, and he wasn't about to start now.

Knowing that the other two bullfighters would be right there turning the bull away from him and the unconscious cowboy, Brant held his breath and hoped he didn't get too roughed up. He had only one night left with Annie and he damn well didn't intend to spend it in the hospital. Or worse yet, be too banged up to hold her, love her one last time.

When a blunted horn connected with his ribs, the air rushed from his lungs and pain knifed through his torso, but Brant continued to cover the fallen man. He was confident the protective vest and padding he always wore under his bullfighting garb would keep him from serious injury, but he was going to be sore as hell before this was over with.

Then just as suddenly as the pummeling began, it ended. The other two fighters had distracted the bull, it ran through the gate leading to the pens behind the chutes, and the sports-medicine team came rushing into the arena to tend to the unconscious man.

"Are you all right, Brant?" one of the physical trainers asked, stopping beside him.

"I'm fine," he said, slowly rising to his feet. He brushed away the dirt the bull's hooves had kicked in his face. "I've got a couple of bruised ribs, but nothing's broken."

"Are you sure?"

"Yep." Brant gritted his teeth against the soreness already seeping into his side as he bent down to pick up his battered hat. "I've had enough cracked and broken bones to know the difference between hurting and being hurt."

Nodding, the man turned to help the others as they stabilized the now-conscious cowboy's neck with a foam collar and lifted him to a backboard.

Brant waited until they'd carried the man from the arena and the overall winner of the event was being announced, before he made his way behind the chutes to find Annie. But before he located her, he saw Patrick Elsworth coming toward him.

"I've been looking for you, Wakefield. I almost didn't recognize you with your makeup on."

"Funny, I haven't been looking for you," Brant said with a shrug. He'd like nothing more than to bury his fist in the pasty-faced little weasel's nose. Then a sudden thought hit him. Elsworth had used his name. "How did you find out my name?"

Elsworth looked quite pleased with himself. "I bribed the desk clerk in Saint Louis and found out who you were and that you're part of this dog and pony show. After that I did an Internet search to find out where the PBR would be next." He shook his little-weasel head. "But that's not important. Where is she?"

Brant didn't even consider pleading ignorance and asking who "she" was. "Annie's where you can't get your hands on her," he said through clenched teeth. "Now, get out of my way before I lose what's left of my temper and kick your skinny little butt."

"Annie?" Elsworth laughed. "Carlotta's going to love that. She'll give you a tongue-lashing you won't soon forget for calling her precious granddaughter anything but Anastasia."

Knowing the man would follow him if he tried to find Annie, Brant started toward the dressing room. Just as he figured would be the case, Elsworth fell into step beside him.

"You know the old lady is the one with the money."

"Do tell," Brant said. He needed to keep the little

weasel moving away from the chute area where Annie was.

Elsworth nodded. "I don't know what Anastasia has told you, but she's just waiting for the old woman to kick the bucket. That's the only reason she puts up with her grandmother's edicts."

Brant wasn't sure who Elsworth was describing. It certainly wasn't Annie. But he wasn't going to argue with him as long as they were moving away from her.

Spotting Colt and Mitch a few feet ahead of him, Brant quickened his pace. When he walked up beside them, he asked, "Colt, do you remember what we talked about earlier?"

His brother looked first at Brant then at the man standing next to him. "Yep."

"I need that favor now," Brant said, quickening his pace.

Grinning, Colt closed the gap left by Brant and put an arm around Elsworth's shoulders. "I think Mitch and I can take over from here."

"Think you can give me about fifteen minutes head start?" Brant asked, breaking into a jog.

"Sure thing, bro," Colt answered, laughing when Elsworth tried unsuccessfully to elbow him in the ribs and connected with his riding vest. "Take more time if you need it."

"Thanks," Brant called over his shoulder.

"What do you think you're—" was all he heard the weasel say as Colt and Mitch hustled Elsworth away.

By the time he entered the dressing room, Brant was out of his shirt and had his protective vest unfastened. Changing in record time, he removed his makeup, packed his duffel bag, then went in search of Annie. He had to get them out of the arena and on the road to their hotel before Colt and Mitch finished detaining Elsworth.

He'd told her that he wouldn't let Elsworth get anywhere near her. And Brant intended to keep that promise or die trying.

Ten

Annie impatiently waited for Brant to fit the hotel key card into the electronic door lock, then close the door behind them. As soon as he secured the dead bolt and turned on the light, she threw her arms around him. "Brant, I was never more frightened in my life," she said, her insides still shaking.

He grunted as if he was in pain. "You're safe now, sweetpea. Elsworth has no idea where we are."

When Brant had joined her behind the bucking chutes at the arena, he'd thanked Sarah for helping to keep her out of Patrick's sight, then hurried Annie to a cab. During the short ride to the hotel he'd explained about his run-in with Patrick. But that wasn't what had her near tears and shaking like a leaf.

"I'm not concerned about Patrick," she said, cupping Brant's lean cheeks with her hands. "I thought my heart would stop when that bull tried to gore you. Are you all right?''

''I'm a little sore,'' he admitted. ''And tomorrow I won't feel like moving too fast, but I'll be fine.''

''Are you sure?''

He nodded. ''I've been in a lot worse wrecks than that little skirmish tonight.''

She watched him place his hat on the shelf in the closet, then slowly remove his jacket. ''Did the doctor look at you after you left the arena?'' she demanded.

''Sweetpea, I'm fine. Really.'' He turned to face her. ''I've got a couple of bruises, but that's it. Promise.''

Blinking back the threatening tears, she hung her jacket beside his. ''Brant, I've never seen anything as heroic as you throwing yourself on top of that downed rider. That was incredible.''

''Nope.'' He reached for her, and wrapping her in his strong embrace, touched his lips to her forehead in a featherlight kiss. ''*You're* incredible.''

It was so like him to minimize his role in saving the cowboy's life. The more she got to know Brant, the more she admired his humble courage.

Annie reached up to unsnap his chambray shirt. When her fingers brushed his firm, warm skin, he closed his eyes and smiled.

''Does that feel good?'' she asked.

''If it felt any better, I'd think I'd died and gone to heaven,'' he said, opening his eyes. His grin held such promise, it took her breath. ''But I don't want to be selfish. Let's make you feel good, too.''

When he reached for the buttons on her shirt, Annie barely managed to stand still as he carefully slid each round disk through its buttonhole. His fingers lingered on the sensitive skin of her abdomen, his touch sending shivers through every part of her.

By the time Brant tugged her shirt from the waistband of her jeans, her heart raced wildly. He pushed the garment from her shoulders, then tossed it to the side and reached for the front clasp of her Chantilly lace bra. "You know, sweetpea, if I didn't know you wore this type of stuff before we met, I'd swear you were trying to drive me out of my mind."

Smiling, she ran her hands over his shoulders, sliding his shirt off as her palms skimmed down his biceps. "Would you have preferred that I bought sensible cotton panties and bras when we went shopping in Denver?"

"Hell, no." He shook his head emphatically. "I'm finding I really like wispy lace and triangles with strings. I'm glad you stuck with them."

From the look in his deep blue eyes, Annie was glad she had, too. But all thought ceased when Brant unhooked her bra, and peeled it away from her breasts. Reaching out, he cupped her in his callused palms, and the feel of his rough hands on her overly sensitive skin set off tiny electric sparks of excitement skipping throughout her body. When he teased her tightening nipples with the pads of his thumbs, she closed her eyes and reveled in his gentle touch.

"That feels good," she murmured.

Opening her eyes, she quickly unbuckled his belt, and popped the snap at the top of his jeans. Her heart skipped several beats when she saw the insistent bulge straining against his fly and a tight coil began to form in the pit of her belly.

"You…um, seem to have a problem," she said, glancing up at him.

His sexy grin and heavy-lidded gaze sent heat racing through her as he lowered his head to kiss the tip of her breast. "I always get this way when I get close to you, sweetpea," he said, moving to take the other tight peak into his mouth.

Her knees suddenly felt weak and rubbery. Reaching out to wrap her arms around his waist, she felt a chill race up her spine at his groan of pain.

"You *are* hurt." Pulling away from him, Annie searched his torso. A huge, ugly bruise covered a large section of his ribs on the left side. Tears filled her eyes as she gently touched his mottled skin. "Oh, darling, it looks awful."

"It's nothing," he insisted.

"It is, too." Taking him by the hand, she led him over to the side of the bed. "Let's make you comfortable." She did her best to ignore the feel of his pulsing arousal as she lowered his zipper and shoved his jeans down to his knees. "Sit down and I'll remove your boots."

Once she'd stripped him down to his briefs, she pulled on her blouse and buttoned it, then grabbed the ice bucket. "Lie back and relax. I'll be right back with some ice." Brant started to protest, but she shook her head. "I'm not accepting no for an answer. You've taken care of me all week. It's my turn to take care of you."

Brant watched Annie remove the key card from his jacket pocket, check the diagram on the back of the door for the location of the ice machine, then hurry out into the hall. The concern he'd seen in her green eyes when she realized he was hurting had sent a warmth spreading all the way to the far reaches of his soul.

Carefully stretching out on the bed, he stared up at the room's textured ceiling. Having Annie fuss over him felt damn good. Almost as good as when he did the same with her. What would it be like to have her with him all the time, taking care of him, making him feel as if his comfort was important to her?

He cursed vehemently and gritted his back teeth against the longing that invaded every fiber of his being. There was no sense wondering about things that would never happen. All they'd have together was tonight. Tomorrow he'd take Annie to her grandmother's, drive back to Saint Louis to catch a flight home, and that would be the end of it. He and Annie came from entirely different walks of life and he'd learned the hard way the two just didn't mix.

When the door opened and Annie walked into the room with a bucket of ice and a plastic bag, Brant smiled at the determination on her sweet face. He'd let her nurse his wounds a little longer, then show her that his injury wasn't nearly as bad as it looked.

"I found a maid's cart and picked up an extra plastic bag," she said, entering the bathroom. Moments later, she walked up to the side of the bed to gently place the ice pack to his side.

He immediately felt goose bumps rise along his skin. "Damn, sweetpea! That's cold."

"Ice usually is," she said, smiling. She sat on the bed next to him. "I'm not very up on first-aid techniques. How long should we leave this on?"

"Not long." He reached up to once again work the buttons free on her blouse. "My thoughts are running in a warmer direction."

"But you're hurt," she protested.

"Take my word for it, Annie. I'm not that bad

off.'' He finished unbuttoning the garment, then pushed it from her slender shoulders. ''My ribs may be sore, but my other parts are working just fine.''

He took the bag of ice and placed it on the night-stand, then sat up to take her into his arms. The feel of her breasts crushed to his chest, her beaded nipples pressing into his flesh, sent his temperature up and chased away any chill he'd experienced from the cold compress.

Reaching between them, he unfastened her jeans and slid the zipper down. ''Why don't you shimmy out of these and get comfortable, sweetpea?''

As she bent to remove her boots, she nervously caught her lower lip between her teeth. A week ago, the thought of stripping in front of a man would have embarrassed her to death. But this wasn't just any man. This was Brant. The man she loved.

When she stood up to push her jeans down, the light in his eyes sent her pulse racing and chased away all traces of apprehension. Never in her wildest imaginings had she envisioned a man looking at her the way Brant was at that very moment. His blue gaze was filled with such heated desire, such hunger, that it caused her knees to wobble.

Hooking her fingers in the string waistband of her underwear, she slowly slid them from her hips and was rewarded by Brant's sharp intake of breath. ''You're the sexiest, most desirable woman I've ever seen, sweetpea,'' he said huskily. ''Come here.''

Annie sat down on the bed beside Brant and when he wrapped her in his arms, the feel of his firm, mas-culine form pressed to her softer, feminine one caused a tingling heat to course through her. Reclining against the pillow, he pulled her down with him, then immediately covered her mouth with his.

She closed her eyes and reveled in the feel of his kiss, but when his tongue separated her lips to entice her with the taste of his passion, heat and light danced behind her closed eyes. His hands on her body, the scent of him wrapping around her, sent shafts of longing to the very core of her being.

As he lightened the caress, he nibbled kisses to the hollow at the base of her throat. "You have no idea how much I've wanted you this way again, Annie," he said, his warm breath teasing her sensitized skin.

"Brant," was all she could manage to get out as he slowly, tenderly ran his hand down her abdomen to the crisp curls hiding her feminine secrets.

Raising his head, he caught and held her gaze as he parted her, then touched her with such exquisite care it brought tears to her eyes. "I love the way you say my name, sweetpea."

Unable to remain still, she ran her palms over his chest, over the ripples of muscle covering his stomach. But when her fingers touched the waistband of his shorts, she smiled. "Aren't you a little overdressed, cowboy?"

His deep chuckle caused a fluttery feeling to tighten in the most feminine part of her. "Why don't you help me take care of that problem?"

When he lifted his hips, Annie carefully pulled the cotton briefs over his strong arousal and down his muscular thighs. Her breath caught at the sight of his overwhelming maleness. But his low groan quickly had her glancing up at him.

"It hurts to move, doesn't it?"

He shook his head. "Not that much."

But she detected the strain in his voice, saw the wince he couldn't quite hide. "Brant—"

Reaching out, he pulled her down beside him. "Sweetpea, I'm not going to lie to you. I'm sore as hell. But I'm not so bad off that I can't spend the night making love to you."

"But how can you—"

His sexy grin sent another wave of goose bumps down her arms. "There are other positions we can explore." He placed a tender kiss on her forehead. "Ones where you're in control and do most of the moving." He paused. "That is, if you don't mind."

The idea of taking charge of their lovemaking caused her stomach to flutter and the coil within her to tighten. Feeling a bit shy, yet excited at the prospect of bringing him pleasure, she smiled. "Will you show me how to touch you?"

She watched his eyes darken with emotion as he took her hand in his and guided her to him. "Sweetpea, I thought you'd never ask," he said huskily.

When he showed her how to caress him, she reveled in the new feelings coursing through her. Never in her entire life had she felt more feminine or more powerful than she did at that very moment.

"Yeah...um, that's it." He groaned, then moved to take her into his arms.

Smiling, she placed her index finger to his lips and shook her head. "No. I'm taking care of you tonight, darling."

Annie watched him close his eyes and tighten his jaw as she explored his velvet skin, the firmness of his desire for her. The feel of him beneath her palm, the strength of his passion, fueled her own hunger, and quickly had her body yearning to give him pleasure in the most intimate way a woman can give to a man. Heat coursed through her veins and the empty ache of unfulfilled need intensified with each passing second.

"Brant...I need—"

Apparently, he understood what she couldn't put into words. "In my jeans pocket," he said, motioning to the pile of·clothes beside the bed. When she retrieved the foil packet and handed it to him, he caught her hand in his and guided it back to him. "Let's do this together, sweetpea."

Helping Brant take care of their protection, she glanced up, and the fire burning in the depths of his blue eyes took her breath. He was handing her control of their lovemaking, and with that his complete confidence and trust. Her heart swelled with more love than she'd ever dreamed possible as she moved to straddle his lean hips and guide him to her.

Annie closed her eyes and reveled in the emotions swirling through her as she took him inside, felt him fill her body with his. A completeness like nothing she'd ever known swept through her and she knew beyond a shadow of a doubt that they were sharing much more than the mere act of lovemaking. Brant was her mate, the other half of herself.

When he placed his hands at her hips, she glanced down into the face of the man she loved with every fiber of her being and lost sight of where he ended and she began. Slowly rocking against him, she felt waves of desire flow through her, and the tension they shared quickly built into something far bigger than either one of them.

Without warning, she felt herself poised on the edge, her body a tight coil of feeling. Wrapped in a haze of need, she heard Brant groan, felt him surge within her as he swept her up and took her with him into the realm of sweet pleasurable release.

Long after Annie had fallen asleep, Brant held her close. He loved the way her small body felt against his, loved the scent of her enveloping him with its sweetness. Hell, he just plain loved everything about Annie.

He sucked in a sharp breath. When had he fallen in love with her?

Closing his eyes, Brant tried to tell himself that it wasn't love, that what he felt for her was nothing more than a deep fondness. But when she snuggled against him and murmured his name, feelings so strong they invaded every cell of his being swamped him.

How could he have let himself fall in love with her? Hadn't he learned from past experience that a woman like Annie could never be happy with a daredevil cowboy like himself? What would he do when she tired of the adventure and excitement and went back to a more cultured way of life? Could he survive when that happened?

His gut twisted into a tight knot. She'd eventually get bored with his lifestyle, and try to salvage what they had between them by trying to get him to fit into her world—something he just couldn't do. Then, how would he ever survive watching Annie leave him?

Brant took several deep breaths in an effort to ease the ache tightening his chest. The answer to that question was simple. He couldn't stand to watch her feelings for him fade as she lost interest in living a simpler life.

Easing her out of his arms so he wouldn't wake her, he slowly sat up on the side of the bed and buried his head in his hands. In his heart, he knew what he had to do. Tomorrow after he took her to her grandmother's, he'd wish her a nice life, kiss her goodbye one last time, then spend the rest of his life wishing that things could have somehow been different for them.

When Brant pulled the rental car to a stop in her grandmother's driveway, Annie's heart sank. This was the last place she wanted to be.

Glancing over at the handsome cowboy behind the steering wheel, she had to blink back tears. Once she got out of the car, Brant would go back to the Lonetree. Without her.

"You weren't kidding about this place, sweetpea," he said, looking around the neatly kept three-story Victorian. "Even the outside looks like a museum."

She nodded. "Normally this type of house looks homey and welcoming from the outside." Staring at the life-size Greek statues peeking their heads above the top of the hedge maze at the side of the house, she added, "But not this one. It's about as warm and friendly as a cold, gray winter day."

"It definitely has a 'keep off the grass' look to it," he agreed, opening the driver's-side door. He walked around the front of the shiny blue sedan to help her from the car.

"Thank you for everything, Brant," she said, unsure of what else to say. "I don't know what would have happened if you hadn't—"

"Don't think about it, sweetpea," he said, placing his finger to her lips. "Everything worked out."

"Have a safe trip back," she said, turning to go inside the house before she did something stupid like throw her arms around him and beg him to let her go to the Lonetree with him. She started up the walk, but to her surprise, Brant put his arm around her shoulders and fell into step beside her.

When she glanced up at him, he smiled. "I thought I'd walk you to the door, and maybe get an invitation for a cup of coffee before I start back."

Annie returned his smile. "Of course." She'd like to offer him more than a cup of coffee. She'd like to offer him her heart. "Would you like to stay for supper?"

Climbing the steps, he checked his watch. "I'm sorry, but I won't have time, sweetpea. My flight leaves Saint Louis tonight around ten."

As she stood in front of the heavy mahogany door with the stained-glass pane, Annie took a deep breath, then pressed the doorbell. Seconds later, Carlotta Whittmeyer opened the door with a scowl firmly in place.

"Where have you been, young lady?" she demanded. "I called the library when I arrived home, but that *child* you have working for you was anything but helpful. She said she had no idea where you were, but that Patrick had been trying to find you all last week." Carlotta stopped to look at Brant, her gaze raking him from the top of his black Resistol to his big, booted feet. "And just who is that?"

"Brant Wakefield, ma'am," he said, offering his hand.

The thin, gray-haired woman's icy glare darted to his hand, then with a sniff, she turned back to Annie. "Anastasia, I want answers. And what on earth are you wearing? You look like some kind of cowgirl in those jeans and that hat. And where are your glasses.''

"It's nice to see you too, Grandmother," Annie said. "Let's go inside and I'll explain everything."

When the older woman stood aside to let them enter, Brant followed Annie through the entryway and into the...parlor? That was the only word he could think of that would fit the room. Dark antiques with heavy brocade upholstery were arranged before an intricately carved fireplace, and paintings in gilded frames hung on the flocked walls. The place gave him the creeps and made him feel as if he should be viewing it from the doorway behind a velvet rope. Following Annie over to an uncomfortable-looking settee, he could well imagine how dismal her childhood had been in this house.

Seating himself beside her, he could feel the tension in her small body, and reaching out, took her hand in his. "It's going to be fine, sweetpea."

"I take it you've been off somewhere with this...man," Carlotta said, making it sound as if he was the stuff scraped off the bottom of boots after a trip through the barnyard.

"Grandmother! Brant is the kindest, most generous man I've ever met. And he helped me when I had no one else to turn to," Annie said, giving him a look that sent warmth racing through him. Reaching into the inside pocket of her jacket, she handed the ring she'd taken from Elsworth to her grandmother. "This is yours. It's what started everything."

"Mine?" Carlotta shook her head. "I've never seen it before."

"It represents several thousand dollars of your

money,'' Annie said. ''Money that Patrick embezzled from your accounts.''

Brant listened as Annie explained what she'd discovered about Elsworth and the threats he'd made. But to his amazement, the old woman completely ignored her.

''Don't you realize the risks you took by going off with a stranger? Haven't I taught you anything?'' Carlotta stopped to send him a narrow-eyed stare. ''Not to mention the damage it could do to your reputation. I can't bear to think what my friends at the garden club would say if they found out you'd traipsed off somewhere with a cowboy.''

Deciding he couldn't listen to the woman another second, Brant rose to his feet. ''Mrs. Whittmeyer, I don't mean any disrespect, but you've got your priorities so screwed up it's pitiful. Who gives a damn what a handful of blue-haired biddies have to say? Annie was in danger from the crook you thought would be the perfect match for her, not me.''

He heard the old gal suck in a sharp breath, then shake her head. ''My granddaughter's name is Anastasia. And this is none of your business, Mr. Wakefield.'' Pointing toward the foyer, she added, ''Please, don't let us keep you any longer. I'm sure you can find the door on your way out.''

Annie jumped to her feet. ''Grandmother, I won't stand for you talking to Brant that way!''

The woman looked thunderstruck by Annie's outburst. He'd bet this was the first time in her life that Annie had openly disagreed with the old gal.

''It's all right, Annie,'' he said, turning to her. He placed his hands on her cheeks and gazed down at her, trying to memorize every feature, every sweet detail of her beautiful face. "Take care of yourself, sweetpea."

The tears filling her pretty, green eyes almost brought him to his knees. "Brant—"

"I have a flight to catch." Lowering his head, he brushed her lips with his, then turned toward the door and walked out without a backward glance.

Once he was outside, Brant walked directly to the rental car and slid into the driver's seat. He had to take several deep breaths in an effort to ease the tightening in his chest before he could fit the key into the ignition and back the sedan out into the street.

The hardest thing he'd ever done was walk away from Annie. But if he hadn't left when he did, he'd have ended up sweeping her into his arms and taking her back to the Lonetree with him. And that would have been a huge mistake for both of them. No, it was better that he'd walked out when he did.

Stopping at a red light on his way out of town, Brant cringed when a bright-yellow BMW barely avoided rear-ending the car in front of it as it slid to a stop on the opposite side of the intersection. He shook his head as he watched the driver impatiently tap his fingers on the steering wheel. But as he watched the man, Brant felt every nerve in his body tense.

It was Patrick Elsworth.

Annie's statement about desperate men resorting to desperate measures suddenly came back to Brant with crystal clarity. Unless he missed his guess, Elsworth was headed for the Whittmeyer place. And if his impatience was any indication, he was about as desperate as any man Brant had ever seen.

A mixture of fear and anger burned at Brant's gut

when he watched the BMW take off like a jackrabbit. No telling what the sorry excuse for a human being planned to do to Annie and her grandmother.

But Brant was going to put a stop to whatever it was before it ever got started. If Patrick Elsworth so much as laid a hand on Annie, he was a dead man. Brant would make sure of it.

Eleven

Brant found a place to turn around and headed back to Annie's grandmother's. Stopping once again at the red light, fear churned his insides and he gripped the steering wheel so hard he'd probably leave his fingerprints embedded in it. What if he couldn't get back to them in time?

"Turn green, dammit!"

Once the light changed, the tires squealed and the rear end of the rental car fishtailed as he forcefully pressed down on the accelerator. He thanked the good Lord above that there weren't too many cars on the road ahead of him as he raced back to Annie. He didn't make a habit of exceeding the speed limit, but he'd do whatever it took to keep her from being harmed.

He saw the BMW parked in the Whittmeyer driveway, and pulling the sedan in behind it, blocked it from being moved. He prayed that he wasn't too late as he jumped from the car and sprinted to the front door. Hoping for the element of surprise, he quietly opened the door and slipped inside.

"Yes, I took your money," he heard Elsworth say threateningly. "And you're not going to do anything about it."

Brant carefully crossed the foyer to the parlor door and waited. Anger burned at his belly and he had to force himself to wait. He didn't want to tip the man off to his presence before he was ready to make his move.

"Yes, I will," Carlotta said angrily. "I'll have you arrested."

"No, you won't," Elsworth insisted. "I have no intention of spending any more time in prison, nor do I intend to leave town. I'm staying right here in the same town with you, and I'll leave you both alone, as long as you and your granddaughter keep your mouths shut. Otherwise, you'll both end up like that old woman in Fresno."

"You killed her?" Annie asked. "How did you do it without the authorities finding out?"

"There are ways," Elsworth said, sounding smug.

"My God, Patrick, how could you do something like that?"

The tremor of fear in Annie's voice turned the anger in Brant's gut to pure fury. He'd heard enough.

"It was easy. I found that certain poisons—"

Elsworth never finished his explanation as Brant clamped a hand down on his shoulder, spun him around and planted his fist in the man's pasty face. To Brant's immense satisfaction, Elsworth went down like a chunk of lead.

"I've been wanting to do that for more than a week," he muttered, flexing his throbbing fingers on one hand while he rubbed his sore ribs with the other. Turning to the frightened females clutching each other on the settee, he asked, "Are you two all right?"

Annie eased her grandmother back against the settee a moment before throwing herself into his arms. "How did you know Patrick was here?"

Brant hugged her trembling body to his. "I passed him on my way out of town." Noticing that Elsworth was coming to, he kissed her forehead, then set her away from him. "Go call the police, while I watch this little weasel."

As Annie went to make the call, Brant stood over Elsworth. When the man sat up and rubbed his rapidly swelling jaw, Brant warned, "Don't even think about getting up or I'll knock you on your butt again. Nobody threatens the woman I love."

When the police led Patrick out to the cruiser for his free ride to the Williamson County jail, Annie closed the door behind them, walked back into the parlor and into Brant's arms. "Thank you. I don't know what would have happened if you hadn't shown up when you did."

"Don't think about it," he said, hugging her close. "A little over a week ago I made you a promise that Elsworth would have to come through me before he laid a hand on you. And I meant it."

As he continued to hold her, Annie glanced over at her grandmother. Normally very outspoken, Carlotta had been strangely quiet during the whole ordeal.

"Grandmother, don't you have something you'd like to say to Brant?" she asked, giving her a meaningful look.

"Yes." Carlotta hesitated, then added, "Thank you for helping us out of this…situation." She slowly rose from the settee, and stepping around Annie and Brant, walked toward the foyer. "I think I'll wait in the other room while you say your goodbyes."

"Grandmother—"

"It's all right," Brant said, placing his finger to her lips. When she started to tell him there was no excuse for her grandmother's rudeness, he shook his head. "She's entitled to her opinion, sweetpea."

"Even if she's wrong?" Annie asked, snuggling into his embrace.

"Yep." His arms tightened around her. "I need to go, or I'm going to miss my flight."

Tears filled her eyes and her lungs suddenly felt as if she couldn't breathe. The thought of never seeing him again, never being held by him, was more than she could bear. "Brant, I love you."

His body stiffened against hers, then groaning, he placed his finger under her chin to tilt her face up to his. She watched him close his eyes, felt a shudder course through him before he looked down at her again. "And I love you, sweetpea. More than you'll ever know." He took a deep breath. "That's why I'm going back to the Lonetree and you're staying here."

Annie felt as if her heart was being torn in two. Brant loved her, but he was still going to walk out and never look back. "Why, Brant?" Old insecurities began to surface. "Is it because I'm not—"

"Don't," he said, interrupting her. "You're the sexiest, most beautiful woman I've ever known." He smiled sadly. "But you're used to art exhibits and concerts, while I'd rather ride Dancer up to the ridge and look out over the beauty of the land, or go play chicken in some rodeo arena with a ton of pissed-off beef."

"But I don't enjoy art exhibits or concerts," she said, trying to make him understand how wrong his perception of her was. "I'd rather watch the wildlife babies playing in a meadow than—"

"I know you think that would be enough, sweetpea. But six months from now you'll be bored and wishing for your old life back." He sighed heavily. "You can't change who you are any more than I can be someone I'm not."

"What happened to make you feel this way, Brant?" She needed to understand.

He smiled sadly. "About ten years ago, while I was still in college, I knew a girl from Boston who thought she wanted the same kind of life I had. But it didn't take long for her to get tired of it. Then she tried to get me to dress up and play like I was having fun in her world." He shook his head. "It didn't work." Lowering his head, he kissed her with a tenderness that broke what was left of her heart. "Be happy, Annie."

Then without another word, he released her, walked through the door and out of her life.

"Is he really what you want, Anastasia?" her grandmother asked as she walked back into the room. "Do you really think you could be happy being a rancher's wife?"

Tears streaming down her face, Annie didn't even have to think twice before answering. "Grandmother, I love him with all my heart, and I've never wanted anything more in my life than to be his wife and live on that huge ranch of his in Wyoming." She covered her face with her hands as the sobs she'd held back broke free.

Carlotta surprised her by crossing the room to wrap Annie in her arms. "Let's sit down and see if we can work this out."

Once her grandmother had led her over to the settee, and settled them both on the uncomfortable couch, Annie accepted the handkerchief Carlotta offered. "I'm sure you heard him." She knew for certain the woman had been eavesdropping and had heard word for word what had been said. "He's convinced that I'd become bored and want to return to my way of life here." Meeting her grandmother's gaze, Annie shook her head. "But he couldn't be more wrong. I've never felt more exhilarated, more alive, than when I was with him on his ranch, or watching him do his job saving bull riders."

Carlotta sighed heavily, then patted Annie's hand. "You're your parents' child." She dabbed at her own eyes with a lace-edged hankie. "I think I've always known that. But I was so afraid I'd lose you like I lost your mother." Smiling sadly, she said, "Can you forgive me for making your life miserable all these years?"

"Oh, Grandmother, I wasn't miserable," Annie said, putting her arms around the older woman.

"Yes, you were," Carlotta insisted. "We both knew it." She shook her head. "But I thought if I exposed you to all the things I found enjoyable, you wouldn't take the risks your mother took. Now, after seeing you with that young man, I know I was wrong." Patting Annie's cheek, Carlotta smiled.

"I've never seen you look more like your mother than when I opened that door this afternoon to find you standing there with that cowboy by your side. There was a radiance about you, a spark of life in your eyes that I hadn't seen since you came here to live with me."

"But you were so…" Annie's voice trailed off as she searched for just the right word.

"You might as well say it," Carlotta urged with a self-deprecating grin. "I was rude."

Annie couldn't keep from smiling back. "Yes, you were."

Carlotta shrugged. "I've been a fool."

"I wouldn't go that far, Grandmother."

"I would." Carlotta took a deep breath. "I was too obtuse to see Patrick for what he really was. But your young man—"

"His name is Brant, Grandmother."

"Brant saw, and as far as I'm concerned, he's proven himself." Carlotta reached out to take Annie's hand in hers. "He may take risks with his own safety, but he would never take risks where you're concerned."

Annie shook her head. "It's probably not an issue now. He made it pretty clear he doesn't think we have a future together."

"Then prove him wrong." For the first time in her life, Annie watched a genuine grin light up her grandmother's wrinkled face. "Show him just how persistent and stubborn a Whittmeyer woman can be."

Grinning back, Annie asked, "You think a Whittmeyer woman with the last name of Devereaux can pull it off?"

Carlotta laughed out loud, the unfamiliar sound

seeming to brighten the room with its rarity. "You were raised by the best. There's not a doubt in my mind that you can bring that young man to his senses." Rising from the settee, she motioned for Annie to follow her. "Come into the kitchen and help me put on a pot of tea. We have a strategy to plan."

Brant stood behind the chutes at the PBR event in Albuquerque, doing what he'd done every second of every day for the past month—thinking about Annie. Hell, he couldn't even look up into the crowd and see a blond-haired woman without having his heart pound against his ribs and his stomach feel like the bottom had dropped out of it. And it had happened again just a few minutes ago. On his way from the dressing room to the arena, he'd seen a little blond walking along with Mitch's sister, Kaylee. They'd been quite a distance ahead of him, but he'd damn near broken his neck trying to run across the smooth surface of the staging area on cleats in an effort to catch up to them.

He glanced over at Colt and Mitch as they went through their stretching ritual in preparation for their rides. And he would have caught them too, if those two boneheads hadn't stopped him to ask advice about the bulls they'd drawn.

Taking a deep breath, Brant shook his head. It was just as well. It would have turned out to be one of Kaylee's friends from college, or the new girlfriend of one of the riders.

When the last of the bull riders had been announced, Brant walked into the arena with the other two bullfighters working the event with him. The surge of adrenaline he always felt when he stepped out into an arena helped to clear his head and he focused on getting through the next few hours. Once he did that, he was going to admit defeat, travel back to Illinois, and wear out the knees on his jeans if he had to, crawling at Annie's feet, begging her to give him another chance.

For the first fifteen minutes of the round, Brant found himself wondering why he was even there and couldn't wait for the night to be over. It seemed that every rider so far had drawn a "union bull"—when the horn blew, the animal quit working and trotted docilely out of the arena and back to his holding pen.

But after those first few rides, all hell broke loose. Starting with the bull Mitch had drawn, every one of them blew out of the chutes like a cyclone. Then, once the rider had been bucked off or had dismounted, the bull turned around and went after the cowboy with blood in his eyes. It kept Brant on his toes and his thinking about Annie to a minimum.

His adrenaline was at peak level by the time Colt's name was called, and Brant knew immediately that something was wrong when his brother tried to dismount. Thanking the good Lord for building him a little taller than most bullfighters, Brant ran forward, leaned over the back of the raging, spinning animal and worked to free Colt's hand from where it had hung up in the bull rope. It took a couple of tries, but using every bit of his six-foot-one-inch frame, Brant finally managed to slip Colt's hand free.

As Colt ran to the safety of the chutes, Brant started to push away from the angry animal, but the bull had reversed his spin and was already turned before Brant could get his feet back under him. Watching the bull lower his head, Brant knew there was no escaping the inevitable. He was going airborne.

Five minutes after being tossed around like a rag doll, Brant found himself lying on a training-room examining table, answering questions about where he hurt and how bad. "I told you, I'm all right," he said for the third time. "Now, give me the go-ahead and let me get back out there to do my job."

"You know the drill," the physical trainer, Ben Wallace, said calmly. "Anytime you lose consciousness, you have to be checked out thoroughly."

"Hell, I didn't much more than close my eyes," Brant argued, starting to sit up. "I was out all of thirty seconds, a minute, tops."

"Brant, stop arguing with the man and let him do *his* job."

Brant's heart stopped, then pounded hard against his ribs at the sound of the familiar female voice. Was he hallucinating? Had he suffered a worse concussion than what he'd thought?

Raising up on one elbow, he looked around, his gaze zeroing in on the woman standing just inside the training-room door. She was wearing a black Resistol, jeans, a hot-pink western shirt and a pair of fairly new-looking boots.

Damn, she looked good. Real good.

"Annie. That was you with Kaylee, wasn't it?" he asked, suddenly feeling awkward.

He wasn't real thrilled with the idea of having her see him like this—laid out on an examining table, his face smeared with a mixture of greasepaint, dirt and God only knew what else. It wasn't exactly the way he wanted to look when he pleaded his case to her.

"You saw us?" she asked, walking over to stand beside him.

"Yeah, for about three seconds, before I was waylaid by the two boneheads," he said sourly.

"Kaylee gave Colt and Mitch strict orders to delay you if you came out of the dressing room before we could get to our seats," she said, nodding.

"You mean, they knew you were here and didn't tell me?" he asked, irritation beginning to burn his gut. The next time he saw his younger brother, Brant was going to throttle him.

She shook her head. "It's not important whether anyone knew and didn't tell you. I'm not here to play games. I have something to say, and you're going to listen, cowboy."

Brant had never seen Annie look more determined. Sitting up on the side of the examining table, he started to put his feet on the floor, but she blocked him by moving to stand between his knees.

"I don't think this is the best time, sweetpea."

"I think it is." She turned to the physical trainer and smiled. "I think this nice man will agree that your injuries are too serious for him to let you leave until after you've listened to me."

"That's right," Ben said, grinning.

Brant glared at the man. "Do me a favor, Ben. Don't help."

Chuckling, Ben headed for the door. "I think I'll go watch the rest of the bull riding."

Once the man left the room, Annie turned her attention back to Brant. "You know I'm pretty darned tired of people telling me what they think is *best* for me." She poked his brightly flowered shirt with her finger. "I'm perfectly capable of making my own decisions."

"I've never tried to—"

"Oh, yes you have," she said, cutting him off. "You decided that you knew what was best for me a month ago when you walked out of my grandmother's house." Reaching over to pick up a towel from a utility cart, she wiped at the streak of dirt along his jaw. "You said you knew that I would get bored and eventually want to go back to my former way of life." She stopped scrubbing his face to give him a pointed look. "Like I'd want to go back to living in a mausoleum."

She seemed to be gaining steam, and he didn't think he'd ever seen her look more beautiful. God, how he loved her.

"Annie, there's something I'd like to tell you."

"I'm not finished yet," she said, shaking her head. "I've never felt more alive in my life than when I was with you at the Lonetree, or watching you risk your life to save bull riders. And I'm not willing to go back to that dismal existence I led before I met you."

"You're not?"

It was all Brant could do to keep from grabbing her and kissing her senseless right then and there. Instead, he gripped the edge of the padded table with his hands to keep from doing just that. He was enjoying this new, more assertive side of Annie and he wanted to hear the rest of what she had to say.

"No. I'm not ever going back to living the way I did before." She turned her cleaning efforts toward his forehead. "A little over a month ago, I met and fell in love with a wonderful man, who has this misguided belief that a woman from Illinois couldn't possibly be happy with a man from Wyoming.'' Finished with cleaning his face, she tossed the towel on the bed beside him, then gave him a look that sent his blood pressure skyward. ''But I'm not going to give up on us without a fight. I'm going to follow this cowboy around like a buckle groupie—''

''Bunny,'' Brant corrected, grinning. Unable to hold himself in check any longer, he reached out to pull her into his arms. ''They're called buckle bunnies, sweetpea.''

''All right, I'll be a buckle bunny and follow him everywhere he goes, if that's what it takes for him to come to his senses.'' She stopped to nibble on her lower lip before she added in a more timid tone, ''And if he really loved me, he'd stop me now and ask me to marry him, before I make a complete fool of myself.''

''Oh, he loves you, sweetpea,'' Brant said. ''Don't ever doubt that. But you were doing such a fine job of reading him the riot act, which he deserves, he didn't want to interrupt.''

Lowering his head, he covered her mouth with his and kissed her with every bit of the love he'd felt since first seeing her shivering on that balcony in Saint Louis. When he finally broke the kiss, her lips clung to his as if she couldn't get enough of him either.

''God, I've missed you, sweetpea,'' he said, kissing her forehead, her cheeks, her perfect little nose. ''Can you ever forgive me for being such a damn fool?''

''Yes,'' she said, sounding as breathless as he felt. ''But don't let it happen again.''

He threw back his head and laughed. ''I take that

to mean you won't let me get away with it, even if I did come up with another lamebrained notion.''

"That's right, cowboy," she said, her smile touching his soul.

Gazing down at her, Brant's amusement faded. "I promise you that I'll never, as long as I live, make another fool mistake like that again." He reached up with a shaky hand to cup her satin-smooth cheek. "You're the most exciting, most beautiful woman in the world, and I won't risk losing you again. I love you more than life itself, Annie. Will you marry me and make the Lonetree your home?"

"Oh, Brant, yes, I'll marry you," she said, throwing her arms around his neck. Tears filled her eyes as she shook her head. "But I don't think the Lonetree ranch house is the place for us."

His heart stalled for a split second, then settled back down. He'd be happy anywhere, as long as Annie was by his side. "Where do you want to live, sweetpea?"

"I want us to build that big log home in your valley," she said, her radiant smile causing his body to tighten. "I want us to watch the wildlife babies playing at the edge of the meadow when their mothers bring them down to the creek for a drink. And every summer evening I want to sit on the balcony with you and watch the sun as it slips behind the mountains." Gazing up at him, her voice softened. "Then, when I have babies with Wakefield-blue eyes, I want to raise them there."

Feeling as if she'd turned every one of his dreams into reality, Brant gave her a quick kiss. "Sweetpea, it will be my pleasure to do all those things. But it's not my valley anymore."

"It's not?" She looked and sounded so disappointed, he felt like a heel for teasing her.

"It's our valley," he said, holding her close. "Our own little part of the Lonetree Ranch."

"I love you, Brant," she said, her voice filled with emotion.

"And I love you, Annie."

She snuggled against him. "I feel like we're about to start an incredible adventure."

"We are, sweetpea." Releasing her, Brant jumped down from the examining table, took her hand in his and headed for the door. "Are you ready to begin?"

Smiling at him, she nodded. And, as he led her from the training room, Brant knew in his heart they were embarking on the most incredible, most fulfilling adventure of their lives.

*   *   *   *   *

Be sure to catch Kathie DeNosky's
next Silhouette Desire,
LONETREE RANCHERS: MORGAN
available October 2003.